WILL THE COXEMAN COME THROUGH AGAIN?

Enemy agents by the dozen have been infiltrating America.

How?

Why?

There's only one man who has the brains and the stamina to find out—and that's Rod Damon, The Coxeman, superspy *extraordinaire*.

And from what the enemy knows, and when it knows it, it is all too apparent that the answer lies close to home. Too close, in fact. Someone in Rod's League for Sexual Dynamics is a double agent, and Rod must uncover him (or her) before *all* his agents are killed off.

Will Rod bare the traitor? Or will the Free World be destroyed?

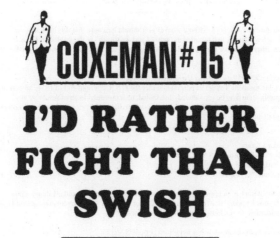

COXEMAN #15

I'D RATHER FIGHT THAN SWISH

AN ADULT NOVEL BY BY TROY CONWAY

POPULAR LIBRARY

Popular Library
Hachette Book Group USA
237 Park Avenue
New York, NY 10017

Popular Library is an imprint of Grand Central Publishing. The Popular Library name and logo is a trademark of Hachette Book Group USA, Inc. The Coxeman name and logo is a trademark of Hachette Book Group USA, Inc.

Visit our Web site at www.HachetteBookGroupUSA.com

First Paperback Printing: September, 1969

Printed in the United States of America

Conway, Troy
I'd Rather Fight Than Swim / Troy Conway
(Coxeman, #15)

ISBN 0-446-54324-1 / 978-0-446-54324-8

CHAPTER ONE

I, Rod Damon, had been challenged.

In the usual, free-wheeling, all-stops-out way. Strictly a case of put up or shut up. After all when a man is world famous for a certain kind of *schtick,* he must learn to expect challenges and know how to deal with them. But I'll tell you one thing, when you are the champ and the King of the Hill, you can't come out second best. Nobody remembers the runners-up.

Especially when your *schtick,* your own thing, is *Sex.* S-E-X. Since I was only the vaunted head of L.S.D.— League of Sexual Dynamics, for those of you happening along late—I had to accept all challenges. Haven't I been telling and showing the world for five long years that a man well-hung, who knows how to use it, can rule a universe of women? My answer for the ills of mankind is getting it and getting it good and plenty. With a platform like that, I am always open to attack. By the skeptics, the prudes, the frightened ones and let's face it—the fakers who just want to get a little for free. All those and the Very Hard Up.

But it was hard to tell about the Puerto Rican *señorita.* More than that. It was impossible to be sure. She shouldn't have had any hang-ups at all. Not the way she was put together.

When she stood up in the seminar I was conducting at the university in one of the many wide, enormous, big-window rooms that always let the sun in, I had to blink against Old Sol as well. But the *señorita,* who turned out to be one Rita Cortez, flung the challenge full into my kisser. Right in front of a class of about thirty of the most prime specimens of the human female animal. My programs on sexual education, designed right after I earned the doctorate in Sexology and rewrote the book, has drawn thousands of willing, panting aspirants yearly. Having released the American female, and the European and Asiatic, from sexual slavery, with my advanced theory of

5

applying ancient sexual mores, customs and techniques to the bedroom department, I had cut quite a swath through fame. I was Rod Damon, America's master of the bedchamber.

So I was in full sail, with a university at my disposal, all the money and food and wherewithal I needed, with an occasional sideline of spying which I will tell you more about later, when Miss Cortez stood up, shook her *maracas* and *castanets* at me and brightly posed her challenge:

"Professor, I dare you!"

"Dare what?" The class snickered, expecting the usual silly bet or challenge: like how many women could Professor Damon satisfy sexually in sixty minutes? I was always being confronted with that old chestnut. It is one of my easiest performances. I can handle as many women as the physical passage of time will allow.

"Will you accept the challenge?"

I stared at her, shaking my head, checked the Delaney cards in front of me for the seating arrangement and the identity of my pupils and folded my arms. The hot sun was baking my face but already my shipping department was warming up on its own. Miss Cortez, who had risen from her seat, would have made Dolores Del Rio strangle herself with her own bra.

"I am a miracle worker, Miss Cortez. But you stump me. Even I cannot accept a dare when I don't know what that dare is."

Now, the class really let her have it. The redheads, the blondes, the brunettes, all the wanton little and big coeds who had come to hear and learn, and perhaps seduce the great Rod Damon.

Miss Cortez did not bat an *enchilada*.

"Dear Professor Damon, it is very simple. Without touching your phallus—without so much as whispering at it—I can make you ejaculate. Fully, completely. *Inevitably*."

A hush fell over the room. Awe registered on all the sweet young things. They were holding their breaths. I could see that. All the rising crests of mammarial wonder thrust out impressively. I *ahemed* and unfolded my arms,

6

assuming my most intelligent look. Miss Rita Cortez stared back at me, from a distance of about twenty feet. Her hair was like night, her lips blood-red, her eyes green flashing fire, and the Snow White image was then uttterly kicked in the pants by a figure Disney would never have dared to show to the kids. *Ai-chee-wow-wah!* She was put together like a brick adobe but not one of those haciendas had ever been so curved, or surging or splendidly realized as a piece of real estate. It was uncanny somehow; I knew she was Puerto Rican because word had gotten around I had one in class and with the name and all, it was an easy guess. But no lady of Latin countries ever had a whiter, more alabaster complexion. Nor such hilly curves.

"Surely you jest?" I suggested.

"No, I do not. Will you accept?"

I smiled. "I have never said No to anyone, dear lady. Not when it comes to any extension of sexual research, knowledge and education. But tell me—for the benefit of your classmates and myself—you seem to contend that you can make me have an emission without coming near my phallus. I want to be sure we understand each other. Is that it?"

"In a word, *yes.*"

Gladly, she was smiling. It could have been mistaken for eagerness or cuteness or just a silly, feminine way to get a taste of Damon but not according to her challenge. The class was hanging on every word now as if we were the only two people in the room, so I decided to play out the moment. In class, I have the taint of the Barrymores. I can act, *too*. It was a fine moment and I didn't want to lose it. Miss Cortez had perked up the program immeasurably. But that smile of hers—it was like the flat smile on an obsidian idol. A rock, a stone, a totem pole. It was a bit chilling. I remembered Miss Cortez very well now. She had gotten one hundred percent on my last examination: *How To Make A Man Make Love In A Chair*. Her answers, her theories, her variations had been startling in one so obviously very young. She couldn't have been more than twenty-one.

"Miss Cortez—" I took the lovely bull by the horns.

7

"There are only seven methods in the world of erotica that can accomplish what you suggest. Seven *known* methods, that is. I know every one of them. If you intend to use any of these ploys on me, I can say without shame, and in spite of my own remarkable physical condition, you would win your bet. So what is the point? If you really only want to get me alone and this is the device you have chosen——" The class didn't laugh as I thought they would. Miss Cortez glared at me from down the aisle.

"I have challenged you, Professor Damon. I have thirty witnesses. Are you backing down?"

"And I have accepted." I shook my head. "But surely, you're not going to submit me to the bull fiddle string attached to the prostate and then twang it—not that old goldie?"

"No," she said, very firmly.

"You're not going to attack from the rear? Anal play which most men can never fail to respond to?"

"No," she said again.

"Then you intend to hypnotize me, fill my mind with thoughts that will make me emit?"

"Certainly not!" She sounded offended.

The class's collective head was swinging back and forth like so many fans at Forest Hills watching the tennis ball change courts.

"Wet dreams are the only really honest method of ejaculation I know for the female partner is not even needed for such fantasy——"

"Please, Professor. Do give me more credit than that. I do not make this proposal lightly."

"Hmmm." I eyed her coldly. "Sodomy then. Well, I'll tell you. I refuse if that is what you have in mind. I can never bend to the will of any other man."

"No. Absolutely no. I will be in the room with you. I alone. And I will make you ejaculate without once touching your phallus."

I frowned. I was running out of methods.

"Ah, I see. The hot oil bathing of the phallus. Of course, now that would do it nicely. Oil, as one sexologist

8

pointed out in his thesis: *Oil For The Vamps Of Asia Minor* has a most salutory effect. Is that it?"

She smiled, but she only shook her head. I was confused at that.

"Not the *seventh* way, then?"

"Yes," she said as lightly as a bird flying across the sky. "Perhaps that way. The *seventh* way. If it is the same thing we are talking about."

I bridled at that. "But that's impossible. You couldn't know that method. You're too young! The secret died with Dealey in London and he passed it on to but a handful of experts. All now in their very old age, I might add."

"You are not old," Rita Cortez said with all the meaning in the world and the class let out its breath. It was an explosion of sound in the big room. Dozens of female hearts thundering, a score and more of feminine contraltos crying out for knowledge.

"*Take her on, Professor!*"

"*Go get her, Rod!*"

"*What the hell is the seventh method? A bag full of feathers?*"

"*I used some marshmallows on a guy once——*"

"*Go get him, Cortez!*"

"*This I gotta see——*"

"*Maybe we should sell tickets—?*"

"*Hot damn! Professor Damon rides again!*"

And stuff like that there. Sweet, honest sentiments all. What else could I expect from a roomful of sex-hungry young things?

"Ladies, please——" I rapped on the desk for silence and order. For a mad second I would like to have pounded with something else.

I stared at Rita Cortez. Now *her* arms were folded, and she was smiling again. The class quieted down but all the Junes were busting out all over. The warm sun made the room hotter than Hades. Easily matched by the more than loaded "pistol" I carry at all times.

I remembered Rita's story. A former Puerto Rican call girl, on the lam from there for some nebulous reason, who was working for a Master's Degree in Sexology. And

9

now she was trying to shame me in front of my class. I held back a smile. We'd see about that. I'd made better dames than her cry out for More with a lot of Uncles thrown in for good measure. Make *me* come without touching me, would she? Hah! She couldn't possibly *know* the seventh method. I'd stake my professional reputation on that.

"All right, Miss Cortez. Game rules. You dared me. I accept the challenge. Any conditions?"

She nodded slowly, choosing her next words with great care. It all smacked of a plan somehow. There was too much cunning in this carnal babe. She hadn't been an *el telephono* girl for nothing, had she?

"Yes, Professor. I should like to conduct this test immediately."

"Sure." I looked at my watch. "I can polish you off before lunch."

Nobody laughed. My sense of humor must have been getting worse. Either that or they *all* were on her side. Miss Cortez stuck out a pink tongue.

"I want the class to watch. From the *living experiments* room. Behind those two-way mirrors on all four walls. It's only fair, isn't it, that they see the way the bet works out?"

"Yes, in the name of research, yes, I suppose." That should have made me irritable but it didn't. I wanted to give this hot tamale her comeuppance before an audience. *Ole!*

"And I want movies made of the test, just in case you should pass out. You know how helpful that would be to future historians in the field? It would mean the opening up of new highways into the dark lands of the sexual jungles of the mind."

I held up my hand.

"Okay, okay. You get a crack at me. Right now. We take movies just in case. The class watches. Fine. But tell me. You have everything to gain, and I have nothing to win, really. Most challenges or bets or dares or what have you, offer some reward for the winner. What do *I* win?"

10

Rita Cortez lowered her lids, almost bashfully.

"If I cannot succeed, Professor—you will be free to enter me in order to do so. That will be my loss. . . ."

"Loss?" I set my teeth, refusing to blow my top. "Dear Miss Cortez, in every quarter of the world as we know it, that would not be considered a loss. Or would you care to consult my fan mail?"

"If you say so." She raised her head, proudly. "Shall we go to the *living experiments* room and begin?"

I nodded my head and that did it. The room was a madhouse of young ladies springing from their bench seats, streaming for the door, babbling like maniacs. There was a flurry of white legs, swinging derrières encased in miniskirts, bobbing breastworks and flying hair. Everybody left books and papers behind before I could stop them. No one even turned around to wish me luck or something. The last to leave was Rita Cortez. She marched from the room like a queen going to her coronation. Or her execution. I wasn't sure which. Our staid old university hadn't had so much excitement and uproar since the day I took the faculty on in the gymnasium swimming pool. The faculty being represented by the O'Hara twins, Miss Jane Slocum and Mary Anne Tidy. They had bet me that a man could not make love in the water. As representatives of the Swimming Class, Music and Drama, I had reacted as only I knew how. I pushed all four of them into the drink and torpedoed them underwater. The O'Hara twins, a sun-browned set of blonde twins, all muscle and curves, nearly undid me that time.

Miss Jane Slocum gurgled something that sounded like the Bell Song from *Lakme* underwater and dear little Mary Anne Tidy, a perky, filled-out brunette, improvised finely and gloriously in the best Method Acting tradition. All in all, things had gone along swimmingly and for months after, the university regarded me with awe. I had given them a living example of Damon in action.

I also got the private keys to each of the ladies' private rooms in the big west wing on the campus. There was no trouble about the O'Hara twins. They were willing to share everything.

11

And now the die was in the cast once again.

Rita Cortez had challenged me. I would either make university history again or fall flat on my . . . face.

It didn't really bother me. I'm one of those happy characters who will do anything for the Lord God Sex. Ask anybody. Ask Walrus-moustache, that autocratic heel with his James Bond missions who was always trying to get me shot up.

Soon I was alone in the big classroom. The girls had raced on ahead. Probably to the wings that surrounded the special room for live research. It was equipped with special mirrors so that outsiders who wanted to watch and take notes or just *learn*, could do so to their secret heart's content. It would do the ladies some good, I decided. They had heard so much about me they might as well see me in action. At my best, as it were. I had no qualms about Rita Cortez winning her bet. I could hold back for a year and a day unless she really knew that seventh method—which I doubted. Dealey had only talked to experts. How could a Puerto Rican girl have learned the method?

I was humming as I left the classroom and locked the door. The long tiled corridor was deserted but I could still smell the assorted perfumes and *eau de* whatchamacallits of my seminar as they had stampeded on toward the Great Experiment. Great Expectations, for most of them. By my personal estimate, at least twenty of the class of thirty were still virgins. Hence, the tremendous excitement engendered by Rita Cortez's bold challenge. The twenty green peas would be shelled on Endpapers Day. Cortez couldn't wait in line, obviously. She was too eager.

I tried not to chuckle out loud. I was going to *San Juan* her to a fare-thee-well when she lost her bet. Make me come without working on me? Working *for* it? *Hah! Hoo-Hah!*

Someone tapped me on the shoulder.

I turned.

I was caught flat-footed, with egg on my face and all my strength to the fore.

A tall willowy redhead, whose willows were bursting to outstretch, threw her arms around me in a bear hug,

12

planted her red mouth on mine, grinded away at my navel with her hips, before letting me go, stepping back breathless and then shoving a long square of envelope into my face. It all happened so fast, I was reaching automatically for the envelope, unable to speak, unable to think.

The redhead's face, all breathless and flushed, her twin assets of chest pumping like pistons, swallowed nervously. Then she suddenly whirled and ran down the hall, her rear end twitching admirably.

"Hey, wait—" I blurted.

"Letter for you, Professor—" she yelled over her shoulder, still running. "I'm Clovis Lee—*I love you, Professor!*"

With that, she was gone. Out of sight beyond the next turn in the corridor. She'd only held me for a second but she'd managed to touch all the bases. On top of Cortez's jungle body and this, I was firmed up enough without a living experiment.

Dumbly I glanced at the envelope. I cringed.

The upper left hand corner bore the printed title of THE THADDEUS X. COXE FOUNDATION. Which meant Walrus-moustache, which meant trouble. Everytime I heard from him by word or deed, my peaceful, Utopian existence was shattered forever. A day later I could wind up in some Godforsaken place like Outer Mongolia. They have women there too, believe it or not. It isn't all yaks. And Walrus-moustache, who is the front man and assignment hander-outer for the Coxe Foundation, has made very prime usage of my peculiar talents many times in the past. The Coxemen pretend to be a dizzy, right-wing outfit in the U.S.A., as a cover-up for their real excuse for being. It is one of the greatest espionage organizations in the country. And so help me, every now and then, Rod Damon is their number one agent *provocateur*. I have done so much *provocateuring* for them in the past that it provokes the hell out of me.

So the letter had to be bad news.

I growled and thrust it into my pocket and bee-lined it for the *living experiments* room. To hell with Walrus-moustache and all the Coxemen of years gone by. I'm a

13

lover not a secret agent. I keep telling them that down at the office. But nobody ever listens to me. Least of all, Walrus-moustache. Him and his World Peace missions. And errands. The only genuine Peace I'm interested in is not spelled that way. And I'll take it and go after it at any price.

Rita Cortez was waiting.

With her stacked deck.

I was going to flip all her cards until she came up cross-eyed Jacks.

Catch me letting some little old college girl put me down. Not even an experienced call girl could get the best of me.

That was my mood as I hummed and whistled en route to the scene of the action. I tried not to think about the Coxe Foundation and that damn letter in my side pocket that looked so important. If Paris was burning and London Bridge was falling down and Rome was toppling and the White House was wired for sound, I didn't care.

Damon had business with a lady.

And that, my friends, always comes first.

CHAPTER TWO

The letter got the best of me first. And then Rita Cortez did. Between the two, I didn't know which end was up. Walrus-moustache is always getting in on the act!

I couldn't help myself. I walked into the *living experiments* room, nodded absent-mindedly to the waiting Rita Cortez and then, so help me, I opened the letter. *I couldn't help myself.* I had to know before I busted a gut what in hell the Coxe Foundation had up its grants this time. As if I didn't know.

I was so preoccupied I didn't undress myself the way I ought to have. The *living experiments* room is right out of a mad scientist movie. The only thing missing is the test tubes and the operating table. Otherwise, it's the same bare, blank four-walled room with couches and sofas and divans. And wall-to-wall rug just for extras to

14

help students and knowledge-seekers to get into the mood. I was well aware that the four mirrored sides of the room practically gave my hidden class some choice ringside seats. I didn't care. The Coxe Foundation's sudden summons was exactly what I expected. With a few variations.

"May I have your tie, please?" Rita Cortez purred somewhere near my ear.

"Be my guest."

"And your shoes?"

"Help yourself."

"Then you'd rather I undress you, Professor Damon? You don't seem very cooperative."

"It's your bet," I said, without really looking at her. "Enjoy, enjoy." I was too busy trying to digest the Mickey Finn the Coxemen had slipped me. So Rita's busy little fingers fluttered and plucked at my outerwear and then my underwear and I was oblivious to it all for a time. The room was soundproof so we were as alone as we could be, save for the hidden sets of twenty-nine pairs of eyes. And Lord knew who else.

The Coxe communication was a humdinger:

PROFESSOR ROD DAMON:
    GO TO THINK TANK IMMEDIATELY THE CURTAIN IS OPENING FOR TOO MANY PERFORMERS YOUR UNCLE IS VERY UPSET THE APPLECART IS READY TO TOPPLE MOVE QUICKLY AND USE YOUR HEAD THIS TIME. URGENT!

                                        WM

It was a coded message, loosely done, but plain enough. I frowned, wondering why Walrus-moustache would even send a letter on such a matter. The Think Tank simply meant I was to report to Headquarters. The curtain had to mean Russia was shooting too many spies into America, and of course, the apple cart was the same old vehicle— *status quo,* world peace. It was a crazy way to get an assignment, I decided. But I folded the letter, put it back into the envelope and went to put it in my pants pocket.

15

And then I realized I had no pants.

Rita Cortez had been busy. Very busy. The shoemaker's elves never had worked so quickly, quietly and effectively. I was down to the buff, all the way down and I had a choice of either eating the letter or shoving it you know where. It didn't matter, really. No one would understand it but me. So I made a paper airplane out of it and shot it for one corner of the room.

Meanwhile, back at my body——

While my mind had been on Walrus-moustache's problem, Rita Cortez had already been to bat and was heading around first base. I was as stiff as per my usual amazing condition but it had nothing to do with her yet. She hadn't so much as looked at it, I gathered. I also gathered something else.

She was sure of herself. Why else would she be wearing a half bra of silken black with brief Bikini to match? Smiling inwardly, I watched her, studying her methods, wondering if she truly knew the seventh method. Any of the first six were good enough for most males but I could have stopped her on those. I have self-control of extraordinary impressiveness. But I had not counted on a Puerto Rican call girl working her way through college to get a lot of knowledge that she would probably certainly use.

She was an eye-opener in the looks and equipment department.

The most perfect figure I had ever seen on a woman. She wasn't dark as you might expect a sun-burned *señorita* from south of all borders to be. She had this inky black hair, the Snow White skin and green eyes that could have brought a million in the window at Tiffany's. But the rest of her rocks were the kind that many a man will smash on in his lifetime. What a coastline! Snug hilly breasts incredibly round and firm, tapering down to a cove of such lambent delight that the ruby of navel above it was like a winking, beckoning eye that shouted: *"Come on in! The water's fine!"*

It was a body carved out of warm flesh and blood and would have made a minister rape a choir singer but I didn't know whether she was frigid or not. Or a nymph

16

or just a daring young lady out for laughs. I could have checked her records; her entrance exam where the university passed judgment on the *psyche* of entrants but it was more fun my way. I always liked to learn about my ladies, in the *field*, as it were. Like this. With the slips down and the skin up tight.

I was right about eighty-five percent of the time, which isn't such a bad loving average.

But Miss Cortez wasn't going to be in that eighty-five. She was to be the Queen of the fifteen.

I could see that almost right away. You can always tell when a dame knows how to take her time milking a cow. Or a bull.

Me, most in particular.

And she very obviously knew the *seventh* method.

Let me give you the blow by blow description.

I stood there and took it all. And then some. She went after me like a dame having her first square meal after years of privation and malnutrition.

I was naked and standing in the center of the room. She was next to me, circling warily, staying miles away from the family jewels but I should have stood in bed. I had a fine full glow on already thanks to my *bete noire* but she simply piled it on like a pro and when she was little more than half-started, my tongue was already hanging out.

She had begun by licking my inner ears. Her pink destroyer was a darting, hot little animal that moved like lightning, flicking and caressing. I have very clean ears but when Miss Cortez willfully was done with that part of my anatomy I was humming like a beehive.

Then she licked my neck, from East to West, traveling like a slow lava bath across the width of my shoulders and pausing every now and then to make me feel the eerily sexy warmth of her breathing. I trembled. I shuddered. I hardened. But I held on, gritting my teeth.

Now she came around me, not looking at me, her eyes intent on my splendid torso. She began to lick and lap and then breathe again and then wash each of my *pectoralises*, or is it *pectorali?*—anyhow, she washed them

17

with her urgent mouth and all sense fled from my skull. I couldn't think of Thaddeus X. Coxe, our dear damn founder, nor could I imagine Walrus-moustache or the true nature of his royal summons. I was on fire. Burning from the toes up and all of Miss Cortez's liquidy, syrupy kisses were touching off fires wherever she went. What was worse, according to the rules of the game, I had to keep my hands off her too. And with all those melting mountains and accessible vales and valleys close enough to eat, I was flipping my thermometer.

And she was only just beginning. I could see that too. She had a million kisses left in her. The seventh method is in a class by itself as something to arouse tired livers. And revive your *libido*.

Now she went after me with a vengeance. Not chewing, mind you, merely butterflying up and down, North, South, East and West, always just a flick of the tongue away from home plate but ever out of reach and never quite touching my most important tendon. My *raison d'etre*, as they say in Sixty-Nine Country. But I was determined to hang in there. I was hanging all right. If she had a coat, a hat and a cane, she could have hung all three on the living tree I was thrusting into the empty space of the room. Also, she was smiling, damn her. Not even working up a sweat. Well, she was going to have to work for me. I closed my eyes, made myself as rigid as a fence-post, which isn't hard for me, and let her continue to strap what I wanted to be, a dead horse. But you just can't fly in the face of Nature, can you?

Even the strongest man has his breaking point.

So Rita Cortez worked all of two hours to find it. Tirelessly, wordlessly, almost effortlessly. As if she had all the time in the universe. I wondered what the thrilled army of females behind the two-way mirrors were thinking. And doing. Sights like these have made *lesbians* and *voyeurs* and just plain carnal babes out of even the most scholastic of women.

So Rita licked on and I wavered.

She lowered herself down my chest, kissing me all the way and then detouring past the hanging gardens

18

to my knees. I trembled, almost going into a lurch but I righted myself in time. I had to open my eyes. Time had lurched on, too. I didn't know how long we had been at it. Later I was to learn it had been all of two solid hours. And I mean solid. I could have hammered ten-penny nails into the floor with what I had going for me.

I had to open my eyes and look down. She was gaining on me.

The top of her ebony haired head was going down, down, down. The lovely curve of her spine swelling into two mountainously shapely buttocks hid the lower half of me. And then it came. The *pièce de résistance* and I couldn't resist it. The last crowning touch that capped off the entire sultry performance.

She flicked her tongue at my bared feet.

She kidded around only for a second and then she planted a full, lingering kiss on the big toe of my right foot.

I came.

Wildly, ungovernably, inevitably, as she had said. A tidal geyser unleashed from my insides, clearing her lovely head and easily reaching the far wall which was a good ten feet away. Man, it was like all the Comings in the world rolled up into one swell stroke. If the room hadn't been soundproofed, I would have sworn I heard a rousing cheer from the opposite sides of the four mirrors.

After that, it was insane.

She didn't stop kissing and I didn't stop coming. The only thing that kept me from flipping her over and stabbing her properly was, as I said, the rules of the game. And all those witnesses. I am a man of my word. And she was a wizard who had won her bet. The seventh way, known only to a handful of experts, had somehow found its way into the brain of a shrewd lovely ex-call girl from Puerto Rico.

I plastered the far wall three more times. If it had needed a coat of white paint, I had saved the university some money. I just stood there and let go as each of Rita Cortez's maddening kisses touched off a fresh blast. I was reduced to trembling, shuddering jelly. Oh, I re-

19

mained my usual robust size and self. But there was a
difference. A subtle one, true. But a difference. The great
Damon had triggered off four times without benefit of so
much as a feeble glance at the source of all his great
strength and power. Quite a compliment for Rita Cortez.

At least, the effort had cost her.

She was on her feet again in front of me, beads of perspiration dotting her broad forehead. The narrow black
strip of bra couldn't contain the surging, heaving bosom
it held captive. One rose-crested mammary looked me
right in the eye. She had gotten some kicks out of her own
experiment. Her Bikini pants clung damply to the exquisite
contour of her pelvic cage. A small victory—but when
you can't win them all, you comfort yourself with things
like that. She'd had a few private explosions of her own.

I bowed.

She laughed. A light, pleasant little chuckle that told me
for sure she'd satisfied some of her own inner desires.
You can always tell.

"You won," I said.

"It wasn't easy," she admitted. "The average man
would have been finished in five minutes. Ten at most.
I'm surprised you were able to keep your feet. It usually
puts most males down on the floor."

"I am *not* the average man. And you are not the average girl. A fair parlay, isn't it?"

"What do you mean, Professor?"

I showed her my own tongue. "I think we're both entitled to some extracurricular activity and research. There
are some things I'd like to show you. After all, wouldn't
you rather get your orgasms in the standard approved all-
American way? It's more fun, besides."

She stepped back quickly, looking down. I had touched
her and both my hands were on my hips. She shook her
head, a sudden look of something in her green eyes.

"You *are* amazing . . . but not just yet . . . I'm not
ready."

"Not ready?" I echoed. "Who are you kidding? Men
had to pay for your favors in Puerto Rico, you *knew* this
seventh method and now you're acting like a heroine in

20

a Victorian drama! *'Good heavens, Rodney, I'm not that sort of woman——'* Quit stalling. I'm the Professor. I call the shots. You will come to my room tonight after Lights Out. Understood?"

She tilted her chin. The green eyes flashed. The loose nipple winked at me again.

"All right, Professor. If you insist."

"I do insist. But don't look so forlorn. You'll have the time of your life."

"You're very sure of yourself, aren't you?"

"Say, are you for real?" I glared back at her. "This thing isn't put together with air and dreams and imagination. Lady, can't you see with your own eyes? The only thing you'll have to worry about is if I don't go clear on through and come out the other side."

She laughed at that, flinging her head.

"You *are* a bull," she admitted. "Like I have never seen. But we have an expression in Puerto Rico. Translated very loosely it says, *'You cannot pass a camel through a needle's eye——'* Do you know that one?"

"Sure. It's Biblical. But, Miss Cortez, I am no camel even if humping is the end of my existence." I turned away from her. "Come on, let's get dressed. You don't want to catch cold, do you? You get an *A* for this little experiment. For effort, execution and research. And a more than passing mark in enthusiasm."

She was staring at the far wall as she reached for her own clothes which were in a neat pile on the floor. It shone wetly.

"You were rather enthusiastic yourself, Professor."

"All the time," I avowed. "Women like you bring out the best in me."

"You cannot bring out the best in me," she said in a funny voice. "You will see——"

"Let me be the judge of that." I had my pants and shoes on now and was going for my shirt and tie. "There is no such things as a cold or frigid woman, Miss Cortez. That you will come to know if you come to my room."

"I will come. I promise you."

"You will," I agreed maliciously. "Now let's get out

21

of here and see what your experiment did to the rest of the class. I wouldn't be surprised if there was an orgy going on back there behind those mirrors——"

There was, of sorts, but it has little to do with Rita Cortez, me or exactly why the Thaddeus X. Coxe Foundation and Walrus-moustache were in such an all-fired hurry to see me.

Little did I know when she licked me that she had started me off on a road which, if it didn't exactly lead to Perdition, did lead to one of those nefarious, incredible, impossible-to-believe assignments that nearly turn the world upside down. Two worlds.

The Peace World and the Sex World.

Sometimes it seems that it is impossible for this staggeringly important twain to ever meet. They are incompatible bedfellows.

But on to the Think Tank.

Back to Rita Cortez later. The dame with all the *frijoles* and *tortillas* in the right places. I wanted very dearly to dance the oldest dance with her. In bed. She was just made for crawling all over—and into. *Si, si.*

I had a Good Neighbor policy I was sure she would go for.

Had to go for.

Any dame that gets the best of Damon deserves all of his undivided attention, it says here.

Besides, I had to find out from her who spilled the secret of the seventh method to her. That kind of important poop should never be handed out willy-nilly to the first comer. Some secrets have to be kept lest all societies lose their esoteric natures. After all, does Macy's tell Gimbel's? No, of course they don't.

"Professor Damon!" the class all cooed in chorus when we got back to the big room with the sun still shining in, "we didn't know you had it in you!"

The sarcasm did not pass un-noticed. I stared back at their flushed, happy, girlish faces and solemnly declared, for the benefit of Rita Cortez, who had returned in triumph to her seat: "You will all write a three-thousand-word composition on the experiment you just viewed.

22

With the exception of Miss Cortez, of course. After all"—
and there I smiled at her to show her there wasn't any
hard feelings except the usual ones— "nobody ever asked
Elizabeth Taylor to write about her wedding night. Or
nights. Such a requirement might deal the institution of
multi-marriages a blow from which it could never recover.
Class *dismissed*. . . ."

A hand shot up in the back of the room.

"Professor! Just a sec—please?"

It was Doreen Doremus. At first glance a candidate for
Weight Watchers, Inc., but for all of her roly-poly girth
and truckhorse dimension, a sweetheart of a young woman
eager to learn about life and men and sex. I always gave
her more leeway than the others because she needed all
the help she could get.

"Yes, Miss Doremus, what is it?"

The class snickered to a woman and I repressed a smile.
She might have been Miss Doremus to me, but to everybody else she was affectionately known as Fat-Ass. Un-
beknownst to the class, unless Doreen had a big mouth,
it was also my love-call nickname for her. You couldn't
do much in the sack with Doreen, but she had a tongue
that compensated for all her shortcomings. She could
speak seven languages and was unable to say *"No"* in
any of them.

"Um—about the experiment—if we write about what
we saw should we put down everything?"

"What do you mean—everything?"

Doreen stalled a second and then her chubby face
grinned.

"I mean the part where you tried to read a letter then
gave up and kind of—you know—*ululated* right in front
of our eyes."

I put my teeth together. Miss Rita Cortez was smiling
down into her notebook, her green eyes dancing.

"By all means," I said in a flat level voice. "Every ulu-
lation, every quiver. The sexual response is what you are
here to understand. Remember that. In Sex, we leave
nothing out. We put *everything* in."

Doreen Doremus nodded rapidly, fairly chortling.

23

"Hot damn!" she exulted. "What a scene! It'll scorch the paper I write on."

The class roared.

But I gathered up my own notepapers and attaché case stiffly and they all did likewise, trooping out of the big wide room once more. They had had a morning to remember. And I had quite a few scores to settle with Miss Rita Cortez.

Operation Cortez would be a lesson in Oneupmanship or as many times as I had in me. And that's considerable. After all, how could I live with myself when an ex-call girl could go around smiling all the time because she had gotten the best of me without opening her legs? It was too damn much of an insult to be borne.

Still there was the Coxeman Foundation and Walrus-moustache's urgent summons. Miss Cortez would have to wait awhile longer. First things first.

But I did pause for a diversion on my way to the Foundation Building to see Walrus-moustache. I couldn't help myself, really. It was a combination of momentary frustration, white heat and the ever-readiness of the equipment I come with. Inevitable, as Miss Cortez might say.

I was passing the clothes locker on the ground floor of the university on my way out of the building and whom should I spy among the coats and hats but Clovis Lee, the redheaded messenger girl who had avowed eternal love. Her back was to me and she was bending over to insert her shapely feet into a pair of galoshes. I suppose she was one of those women who carry umbrellas even on the sunniest day. I didn't stop to ask her. I was on point and she was the Target For The Moment.

I charged, without even giving her time to turn around.

I was right about her. A tall, hot number. The mini-skirt I deftly hooked up past her waist revealed the smoothest, barest, most inviting set of twin hills in all the feminine topographical landscape. I didn't think, didn't ask, didn't even stop to introduce myself. Before she could straighten up from inserting her dainty feet into the galoshes, I had her nailed. Right up to the hilt in one accurate, well-timed stroke. She shuddered from the im-

24

pact, stiffened into a vibrant velvet wall of lush target and without even turning around, breathed huskily. "Anything, Professor, *anything*. . . . I am yours . . . I can't wait a moment longer. . . . Oh, I knew it would rain today!"

Whether she was speaking figuratively, euphemistically or was just one of those women who have to have poetry with their jollies, I didn't know or care. I felt like a man again, sheathing my lance and dipping it into the honey barrel of living.

We pistoned rapidly up and down, back and forth and despite the cramped confines of the clothes locker and the blood rushing to her head, she did just fine. She was more than willing and eager. She was also quite skilled. Very few women in the universe have the full knowledge to know that when they are being Greeked in the classic style, it is quite proper and extra-nice to reach back and gently encircle the bouncing balls with their lily-white hands. Clovis Lee knew how, though. A most rewarding student. She had obviously paid attention in some of the Open Seminars I had given in the Main Hall.

"Ah," I said. "I feel better already."

"Mmmmmm," she intoned in a dizzy croon. "Ain't it the holy truth!"

It was all so sensible and uncomplicated. When I had finished, I put my self together, thanked her and stalked from the clothes locker. She said *"You're welcome, I'm sure"* and went back to buttoning her galoshes. We hadn't looked at each other once. Nobody had interrupted us and all the trials and travails of this mad universe had fled for a brief, enchanted time. I admired Clovis Lee for her civilized outlook. For taking what came with a smile and without explanation or apology. I made a mental note to look her up again. She was prime and the barrel of delights was an untapped bonanza for future improvisations. When I thought of all the things and gambits we could try, my mind boggled.

I don't like to generalize but I've always found redheads a cut above their sisters in the bedroom mentality; they are as free and as blazing as the fires in their tresses.

But don't quote me. I don't want to lose the blonde and brunette trade, either. I'm speaking of natural redheads, of course.

When I finally did arrive at the Foundation Building, it was to be greeted by a steaming, furious Walrus-moustache. He had fairly ripped off the ends of his huge, drooping moustache in agitation. His bright eyes were snapping mad and for once, I did feel a little guilty about not dropping everything and coming running. Usually, it is he who walks in on my love life (at least six times he's found me in the sack when he's dropped assignments in my lap) but this was one time I had all my clothes on when I saw him after a long break between cases. But he was obviously in no mood to appreciate my sober, sedate condition.

"Where have you been?" he growled, taking my elbow and piloting me deeper into the environs of the building. "Dammit, Damon. There are some things that are far too important even to allow for your blasted research into the sexual jungles of the human mind!"

"Says you," I snarled. "And if there are you gotta show me!"

So he showed me.

CHAPTER THREE

Growling and *harumphing* all the way, Walrus-moustache steered me into a darkened screening room. We were alone. The room was somewhere on the ground floor of the Foundation, attended only by an unseen man hidden someplace in the projection room behind a bank of velvet-cushioned chairs. A dim light glowed from a tiny window. Walrus-moustache *sans* his usual bowler hat was still as impeccable as ever. He fathers me to death but is really quite fond of me. I had already proven many times over the wisdom of his judgment in making use of a sex-fiend like me in affairs of espionage. My track record is almost as good as my bedroom one. And that's saying plenty. I have covered Walrus-moustache, the Coxe Foun-

26

dation and myself with glory. Ask your local Secret Service man.

Walrus-moustache gestured me to a back seat in the room and I took it. He sat down next to me with one chair space between us. His eyes were no longer angry. Just sad and troubled. I expected the worst. He rarely disappointed me.

"You may smoke if you like, Damon."

"Gee, thanks."

"We are about to view some movies. Some——"

"Cartoons, I hope. Haven't seen a Mickey Mouse in years."

"—some very important film," he continued, without getting madder. "It is important you be filled in immediately, Damon. There is an *imbalance*."

"There sure is," I agreed. "You need a barber real bad. One side of your walrus is lower than the other. Tsk, tsk. Where's your sense of neatness? Tidiness?" I enjoyed needling him. He is a pompous bastard at all times, despite his intelligence and compassion for the human race. A swinger, too, when he let his moustache down, as I had found out in the fickle past.

"Damon, Damon," he sighed.

"Walrus-moustache, Walrus-moustache," I too sighed.

He leaned toward me and the muscles in his jaws bunched out. His eyes had grown uncommonly cold. I decided to lay off the gags. You can push anybody just so far.

"Listen carefully, you cockhound," he said in a deadly clang of authority. "I have never appreciated what you call wit nor can I ever condone your extraordinary capacity for Sex. Five will get me twenty you are late now because you paused to pluck another of your very willing flowers. All well and good. I admire that in you but I also know the day and time may come when it will cost you your neck. That *real* neck that spans your head and shoulders. So do cut the comedy and pay attention. You've nothing to lose but your life. Do you understand me?"

"Loud and clear. I should leave the wisecracks to Johnny Carson."

27

"Quite. Now——things were going fairly smoothly. Nothing big has loomed, as it were. No bombs, no assassinations, no overt threats that we have to deal with. But there is something far more subtle and nebulous going on. Something we shall have to give our time and thought to before it blossoms into something too big to handle. And above all, we must be ready for it when it comes. Which is why I have asked you here to see this special film. I'll elaborate later, of course, but I want you prepared a trifle for what you are about to see. Did you understand the nature and import of my message?"

He was one of those people who say everything twice. I told him what I had divined from his coded note. I do much better on singing telegrams.

He nodded, pleased. I was learning all the time, he obviously decided.

"Very good. There's hope for you yet. Yes, that's about it. Our Russian friends have upped their quota it seems. Ye Gods, it's like the old Immigration Years—Statue of Liberty and all that."

"And you called it an *imbalance?*"

"Yes," he sighed. "We've checked it out here. Our own agents and records. No doubt about it now. There has been a sudden influx of enemy agents coming into the United States. A staggering number, really, given the quietude of conditions now. All our intelligence agencies are very worried. The CIA is upset, the FBI is perplexed and the Immigration people are totally bewildered. There is no explanation for it. You know how the *status quo* is between this country and Russia. We pretend to be friends, both looking for world peace, but how can we ever really trust them? God alone knows what goes on in those millions of square miles behind Moscow. Not to mention their awful habit of constantly supplying hostile nations with weapons and wherewithal. You see what we're up against? Why all this sudden fresh trafficking in spies? Why are they inundating our landscape with buggers with cameras and codes and shortwave radios? We have to know, Damon. There's no way out of *that.*"

"So what's it got to do with me?"

28

I braced myself, thinking of Russian winters and frost-bite and brainwashing and Commie torture camps. My penis began to feel like an icicle. Brittle, and very, very breakable. And cold.

"Patience, Damon, we have to see the movie first. This has been an informal briefing."

"Wait a minute," I frowned. "Russia has enough agents in the good old U.S.A. Maybe——"

"Ah." Now he really smiled proudly. "You begin to see the point. Exactly. Our spies seem to be Russian but what if they are not? Perhaps they are merely *provocateurs* or saboteurs or worse. That is our only other alternative. That these agents flooding the country are *not* Russian. If not, then what are they? Who are they?"

"You're asking me? All I know about spying is what I get from those lousy movies. You know, all those great dames and gadgets——"

"Damon, Damon. Do not demean yourself. You have proven your worth as an agent many times. A trifle unorthodoxically perhaps, but who's to quarrel with success?"

"You say. I say I was lucky and you know it."

"As I said—perhaps—but I refuse to break up a winning team. We have come through in the past. We shall do so again."

"You sound like a recruiting poster," I rasped. "Let's see the movie, huh? And I'll try not to hate you for not bringing the popcorn."

He chuckled and turned to wave his hand at the hidden projection room man. The dim lights in the room blacked out altogether. We both settled down. No further conversation was necessary. I folded my arms and tried to look intelligent. It wasn't easy. My mind was busy with memories of Clovis Lee's downhill glory, with sensory imaginations of Rita Cortez's potential. I already knew about her miraculous tongue. Not even Fat-Ass Doremus was in her class as a lapdog and Doreen was no slouch at all. I thought about my class of girls too. Thirty, count them, thirty. Surely among all that wealth of female fineness there were——

29

What the hell did I really care about Russian spies? Or any kind of spies? We taxpayers pay damn good money to keep the FBI and CIA in clover and coffee and cake to take care of such things.

My mood was not good as the screen flickered alive and Walrus-moustache's documentary-type film came into view. Already I felt like the nastiest movie critic in the business. Prepared to hate and dislike whatever I saw. I was in no mood to hand out Oscars for anything. Least of all to a bunch of government agents or Coxemen who had rounded up about ten thousand feet of very special film detailing all the gadding-about and mysterious machinations of a bunch of nameless unknown men maybe known as Joe Spy. Who needed it? Spies Under Surveillance!

For that's exactly what Walrus-moustache's sneak preview turned out to be. I felt like I was seeing *The House On Ninety-Second Street* all over again. That one was a pip—remember? Lloyd Nolan and all his Feds cracking a spy ring in little old New York during World War Two. This was the same kind of photography, same kind of catch-the-spy stuff.

Only I'm not Lloyd Nolan.

Even watching all that spy-type footage of film left me bored and restless. After all, looking at pictures of nondescript types walking down streets, going in and out of restaurants and hotels and taking cabs and all that gook isn't exactly like watching a good adventure movie like *The Adventures Of Robin Hood* or a fun show like *King Kong*. Hell, there was hardly one dame agent in the crowd unless one of the spies was in drag. So it wasn't even a hot film like *I, A Woman*. That sort of thing might have interested me. Might, I said. As it was I was only treated to a long, drawn out now-you-see-them-now-you-don't type of film entertainment. I was bored sappy.

It looked like Moustache Man was right, through and through. There were enough enemy agents in his home movie to fill a ballpark for a World Series game. Tall, short, fat, thin—every kind and type there is. I spotted one character about six feet six and one no taller than Mickey Rooney. They had tapped the barrel all right.

But as I said a real turkey movie. I wouldn't have given it two stars in my sleep.

There was only one interesting item in the whole grab bag of spies. Only one odd and unusual factor that held my interest and made me crane my eyes at various points of the film.

The first time each agent photographed wandered on screen, I was immediately struck by an oddity, which might have been a color imperfection but then it became rapidly clear it wasn't.

Each and every agent, I lost count how many there were—had a sunburn. A strange kind of sunburn. Not the kind you would get from an ultraviolet lamp or five weeks at Miami Beach, either. No. It was more like the sort of windburn and flush you see on guys who come back from a long tour in some naval base close to the North Pole. Or a season in Siberia. The way Admiral Byrd always looked. Remember?

Bronzed, tanned and somehow bitterly-cold looking. *That* kind of tan. It was out-of-the-ordinary that all of Walrus-moustache's filmed actors could look like that.

Finally the film was over. Around about my fifteenth yawn which I manfully tried to stifle. I didn't want Walrus-moustache to get sore at me all over again.

The dim lights went on after the screen went blank and he turned in his seat to look at me.

"Well?" he challenged.

"It will never get booked at Radio City Music Hall. No love interest."

"If this master plan goes through," he said acidly, "there may never be a Radio City Music Hall. Think about that, funny fellow."

I didn't have to. I stopped making with the jokes.

"I did see something unusual. You notice all those suntans those fellows had? That kind of windburn—" I went on to elaborate and his eyebrows shot up. For a long second, he frowned. Then he smiled.

"Really, Damon. All your worth is *not* in your pants.

31

You are absolutely right. I saw that too—but I didn't pay any attention to it as you did. I imagined I was seeing Russians and I took their shade for granted! Moscow winter and all that. Splendid, dear boy. Splendid!"

"Will you stop sounding like an English movie?" I growled. "What are you going to do with me?"

"I'm not sure. That's why I wanted you to see this film. I want your ideas on the subject."

"Good. I've got a couple."

"May I hear them?"

"If you don't, I'll collapse into tears."

"All right, all right," he lowered his voice. "Out with it. What have you come up with in that tricky mind of yours?"

"Just this. Ask all our allied agencies to help with the problem. The works. The CIA, the G-Men, the Secret Service, Interpol—all of them. Ring up Europe and Russia and toss everybody into the pot. That way you'll have thousands of eyes on the lookout. How does that sound?"

"Commendable. We'll have to do exactly that, really. I can't see how it's avoidable. They'll cooperate too. Nobody wants a nuclear holocaust. And your second thought?"

"That strange windburn. I don't have to go to Russia, do I? What can one man accomplish in somebody else's ballpark? Keep me here. Let me work on that angle right from the university. I have an idea how to set up a proper spy ring—all those students of mine. They'll think of it as a lark and nobody would ever suspect them. Besides—"

I said icily, "I do not want to freeze my nuts off in that Godforsaken icebox."

He chuckled and shook his head.

"Even for a Coxeman like you, that plan is, to say the least, unorthodox. But——"

"Say yes and I won't make any more bum *bon mots*."

"You always break your promises. Your stiff penis has no conscience. Or character."

"Never mind that. Yes or no?"

"Yes," he hedged. "For the time being, at any rate. I had no cogent idea as to what to do with you in this

32

enterprise anyway. At least, you've come up with something. I have not. I'll take the consequences."

"Bully for you," I said, extending my hand. "You're all heart."

"Please." He shuddered. "What an opening."

I ignored that, got to my feet and stretched. I almost poked his eye out. With an arm, I mean. He glowered and fingered the scruff of his favorite hairpiece.

"I beg of you," he warned. "Just be discreet and careful. And remember how important this is."

"You're a grown man. You don't have to beg. And haven't I always done the job?"

"Yes, you have," he admitted. "But don't you dare tell me you haven't had a ball, Damon. My God—when I think of the Olympics, Sarmania, Puerto Rico and that Venus woman and the *Academie Sexualité*—you have gone to the well many times, my friend."

"Well?"

"Oh, get on with it," he growled. "Call me when you get your hands on something—I mean when you have a piece of—" He gave up, spreading his arms. "When you *know* something, I should like to hear it."

I grinned. "Scout's honor."

"No," he said. "I want your word as a Coxeman. You are not a Boy Scout."

"As a Coxeman," I said stiffly. "You have my undying pledge."

"Mmmmm." It was all he said.

I left him then, with his blue funk, his film footage and his very busy mind. He remained in the chair, snaffling his moustache. I quietly left the movie room.

The film was over, the assignment was on and I had some plans of my own.

But I never was one to rush things.

Particularly when I have rolling in the hay in mind. Russian spies, world peace and swollen immigration quotas and strange suntans could wait at least another twenty-four hours. I am still an instructor and a professor in the field of sexology.

And there was still a world-full of hungry, eager-to-

33

learn students ready to surrender their fresh young minds and bodies to my knowledge.

As I left the Foundation Building on my way back to the university, I put in my thumb and pulled out a plum from my mental pie. It was still too early to collar Rita Cortez but there was a Clovis Lee awaiting and apining. Rita was supposed to come after dark, in the evening.

Clovis Lee.

I would be her General Grant. She could surrender to me all over again. Her backside had been a valley of fun and games and a ball but now I was rather anxious to attack the problem from the front. Visions of red hair, freckles and peaches-and-cream flesh danced in my head. I whistled a happy tune on my way back to the classroom.

Not that I felt afraid.

How could I?

The King and I were one and the same person.

And you *always* see us together. . . .

Behind the locked door of my special suite of rooms at the university, Clovis Lee stood naked in the center of the room. The slight interlude in the locker room had not deceived me. She was a strawberry roan all the way. Long, wide flanks, hilly haunches, an upsweep of two breasts that would knock anybody's eye out. She had her eyes open and was standing at attention. Arms flat along her thighs. She was built like a deluxe, streamlined hourglass. With sands that shifted and filled out with each tremor of her body. Willowy she was but sturdy.

I circled her warily. I was bare-assed naked too.

After all, I don't learn something and then discard it so easily. That is not the role of the true seeker of knowledge. I'd gotten an afternoon pass for Clovis Lee so that she could study privately with me until sundown. Or as long as I wanted her to. The university yields to me in all things. After all, I put the place on the map.

"Professor," she moaned softly. "Do we have to wait? I'm kind of anxious—"

"Me too. But I want to try something."

"Try!" she moaned. *"Try!"* She was writhing, poor kid.

34

Small wonder. The eighth wonder of the world was in view and the fact that it would be all hers any second now had kind of staggered her.

"Be patient. I must kiss you first."

"Where? Where?"

"Don't move your head. Stand perfectly still. Don't touch me. I won't touch you. Not with my hands any-way——"

Her tongue was already hanging out. Shades of me and Rita Cortez. I felt sorry for her so I began. Rushing it just a little. I didn't want her fainting on me and she looked close to the edge already.

So I kissed her. First on each mammary, rolling a wide arc up to her throat and then around to her ears. When I bit into the lovely lobe of her left ear, she cried out in real pain as if I had knifed her. She swayed. I looked her over. A field of glorious goose pimples had stippled her gorgeous flesh. Her pelvic cage was bumping and grinding into outer space, longing for contact. But the kid was a trouper. Not once did she spoil things by trying to grab me. Her body changed from gooseflesh to damp-ened, throbbing, vibrantly torrid skin. I lowered my mouth to her navel and began to slide down, keeping my own hands locked behind my back and my armament away from the glory hole.

It was too much.

For both of us.

I was as bored now with experimentation as I had been with Walrus-moustache's movie. I didn't want to prove anything in particular. All I really wanted to do was get laid.

So—I laid her.

Or rather, her resolve broke, her control skipped out the window and she went berserk. She got me first. Before I could unlock my hands or take up a stand.

She murmured a low growl, like a tiger in the bush, and lowered her own head and charged. I don't know how she did it but before I could say Howdy Doody, she had scissored her thighs apart, meshed gears and swal-lowed everything I was putting on the table. In one swift, flooding sensation of glory and majesty, we were melded into one whole. Face to face, chest to bosom, cheek to cheek. She gave one awesome grind and bump, closed around me like a clam, and standing there in the center of the room, we both must have rocked the building. I am used to many things, many beds, chairs, doorways, all kinds of positions but seldom had I enjoyed juicily and joyously, the old familiar stand-up quickie jet-job which dates back to the London streetwalkers of World War Two. After all, those blackouts due to nighttime bombing raids by the *Luftwaffe* opened up a whole new field of research. War, damn its existence, does bring out the best from the worst sometimes. Look at Penicillin, sulfa drugs. . . .

Clovis Lee bombarded me good and hard. And often. She didn't get tired either. The way she should have. Standing like that is awfully wearing on the backbone. Not to mention the forebone.

But she didn't care. She loved me, like she had said.

"Kissing's all right," she huffed and puffed, "but it will never take the place of this . . . oh, Rod Damon, darling . . . I love you, I love you!"

For each declaration of deathless love, she rewarded me with one shocking orgiastic deluge of herself. It was like the flood and my ark held its own. She could never sink me and she knew it. That was why her eyes were so deliriously happy.

I pinned her flanks with my fingers, boring further into the marshy recesses of wonderland.

"There's a big wide bed inside," I said. "Would you like me to show you the Australian Method?"

"Anything," she crooned. "Anything."

"It's a crawl. Like in swimming. Then there's the Host Style where you are my guest and—" I began to fling her toward the bedroom, still attached to her as it were. She closed her eyes, sagging against me, her buttery, warming body a part of me. That's the way it goes when the going is always good.

"Host style, crawl-style, dog-style—I don't care!" she

36

screamed. "Do with me as you want. I'm your slave. Your love slave, Professor!"

Women. Ah me. I must confess, boys and girls, that is the way it is with all ladies and females and women and tiger lilies and sweet wholesome Wandas the world over. Sue, Tina, Mary, Alice, Ruth—you name it. You please a woman in the sack and no matter who she is or what she is, or how young or how old, or what she says and what she doesn't say—*she's all yours!*

Maybe those characters on television will walk a mile for a Camel, but a woman, any woman, will do much more to get her ashes hauled properly. The man who can satisfy a tomato that wants to be pickled has the key to the city. All the cities. Even very great ladies who should know better have never been able to turn down the chauffeur or the flunky once she finds out he has the stick that does the trick. If you don't believe me, tough.

But let me ask you.

The next time you see a beautiful dame in the company of one enormously ugly man and the slob isn't rich, just ask yourself what the Princess is doing out with the stable boy.

At night all cats are gray, they say.

But there's a big difference in cats too. The cat who can out-Tom the other ones is the cat that will be remembered.

Clovis Lee must have been reading my mind.

By the time I had stretched her tall, limp loveliness out on the big bed and climbed aboard, beginning the Australian Method which starts at the painted toenails, she was purring like a tabby.

A big sweet beautiful pussy of pleasure.

"Professor . . . ?" This as I worked my way artfully from right field.

"Yes, Clovis honey baby darling."

"Do you think I'm a wanton?"

"The idea!" I began to surround the burning bush. She sighed and moaned some more but her mind was still on something. I waited only a moment longer.

"I mean—please, tell the truth. I'm so young and you're

37

so experienced . . . and I've got the pills and all the devices back in my room and all the books on the subject . . . but darn it, Professor, I'm just *hot* . . . all the time. I want it nearly everytime I can think of it. Is that bad?"

"Only if you don't give in to it. You want to get headaches and aching kidneys and nausea and frustrations that will turn your food to acid? Nonsense. Being like this —free, eager and responsive—you will lead a happy life. I, Damon, tell you this."

Her thighs twitched as she felt the probing tip of the instrument of desire searching for a resting place. Her breasts did a rhumba of delight, her hands came down trying to hang onto my scrotum again as a sort of guide and escort into the inner sanctum. I let her.

"Gee, Rod . . ." She sighed and kicked her legs until she had me signed, sealed and delivered. I was swelling like a balloon. "You *do* understand. What a man you are. It's so nice to meet you properly after only seeing you in the hall so many times. I've wanted you until my breasts ached!"

"Clovis—" I had reared back for a second, ready for that tremendous first all-the-way plunge that has rolled lady eyeballs from New York to Bangkok. "What color are my eyes?"

"Gee—" The question threw her. "Blue, I guess?"

"They're brown," I said. "Satyr-brown. And you make my testicles twitch. And any woman that does that gets the full treatment."

"The full treatment?" Her voice quavered with delight. She tried to sit up. "What's that? I'll do anything with you like I said but you could give me a little hint—"

"No. I'm going to give you a big hint."

"Oh," she said and subsided back against the pillows, lovely thighs arched wide, ready, willing and waiting. And entirely able to take the full payload. She was built like the Panama Canal.

It's not always easy on them. The first time. Suddenly finding themselves, literally invaded as it were, by the choicest tenderloin in the male league, does have its shock value. Some of them are just too small—in the beginning.

38

"Clovis, count from ten to one. A countdown. Ten, nine, eight . . . you know."

She did as I told her. Breathlessly, quickly, a little rasp in her voice like she was having a hard time breathing. The old anticipation ploy. By the time she got down to one, she was all aquiver with expectation and squirming like a lovely eel. It works most of the time. Milady's imagination is the biggest help of all, sometimes.

I went in, thrusting like a rocket booster, shooting, propelling a missile as guided as anything they have down at Cape Kennedy. The moon shots are just as good and just as perfect and yet not nearly as nice as far as boys and girls are concerned.

Clovis Lee went into orbit. She skyrocketed, trailing sparks.

I followed, putting aside for a few hours, the gory mess of Walrus-moustache and his worries about the spies who had come to take over America.

This was my kind of coming.

It was just as well that I made my arrangement with Clovis Lee. Rita Cortez never did show up that night. Oh, not that she chickened out or changed her mind. Maybe I'm stronger medicine than even I think.

A note was slipped under my front door about six o'clock. That was while Clovis Lee was in my shower, washing down her prime body for some more instruction from the head of L.S.D. The honey was insatiable and I was too happy to fully care about broken appointments. I'd practically forgotten about the torrid lady from Puerto Rico. Until the note brought me up sharply.

It was brief and very much to the point:

PROFESSOR DAMON:

WILL YOU GIVE ME A RAIN CHECK POR FAVOR? I HAVE COME DOWN WITH THE HONG KONG FLU. I WOULDN'T WANT YOU TO CATCH IT CONSIDERING WHAT AN IMPORTANT MAN YOU ARE. THE CLASS

39

WOULD NEVER FORGIVE ME. TILL WE
MEET AGAIN? I'LL BE LOOKING FORWARD.

RITA CORTEZ

Well, there was some measure of balm in that, after all.
The class was bound to think that a mere sampling of
Damon had unnerved the poor young thing. I didn't care.
There was always *mañana* when it comes to affairs of the
body.

Whistling, I tore the note into tiny shreds and went
back into the bathroom to help Clovis Lee pick up the bar
of soap she had dropped.

There is nothing slipperier than a bar of soap when you
are jockeying for position in a porcelain tub.

"I dropped the soap, Professor."

"Pick it up."

"I'm trying to—it's so slippery."

"Try again. I'll steady you, Clovis."

"All right—" She giggled and bent down.

I steadied her.

Her slender fingers closed over the elusive bar. It
skidded once more. She squealed and reached further over
for it. When her grasp finally had the thing pinned and
trapped, I complimented her the best way I knew how.

I fixed my position and lost my head again. Man, but
that woman was glorious from behind.

"Ohhhhhh, Professorrrrr!"

Like I said, she had everything going for her.

"If you're a real nice girl," I said. "I'll wash your back."

I did.

And she washed mine.

And I washed hers again.

And then we repeated the whole routine.

I can't talk about sin and morals and the corruption
of the youth of the day on any actual critical basis but I'll
tell you this much—Clovis Lee and I had to be the two
cleanest lovers in the whole damn world.

Where there's life, there's hope.

Where there's kicks, there's soap.

40

CHAPTER FOUR

As carefully as I select for experimentation in the sexology field, I was even more choosy the next day. Walrus-moustache had given me the green light on my idea of tracking down the too-many-spies affair. So I was on my own. He had gone back to the Foundation to arrange his own matters. I had the university at my disposal. I had thought hard all night long, despite being kept busy by Clovis Lee, who hungered to know all the methods in the book. Came morning and my mind was made up. I had settled on the choices of seven particular students. Five girls and two boys. I decided on some men to help just in case some muscle would be needed. There are times when not even two big tits can match two big fists. You can never be sure in matters of espionage.

So in a private session in my very own bailiwick, I summoned the seven willing lambs. Oh, they were willing all right. When Damon calls, everybody wants to get into the act. The girls, for obvious reasons, the boys because men can always learn from me. My reputation is as staggering in my field as Howard Hughes is in monetary matters. I'm the Bedroom Billionaire. And I am not bashful, either.

My choices were Doreen Doremus, Adele Ash, Corinne Murphy, Norma Davis, Alice Potter and Pete Porter and Tony Eden. All of them were young, healthy, still under twenty-one and raring to grab at life. Just the sort of kids I needed. They were easy to pick too. Once I had them all camped around my room, sitting in chairs, squatting on the floor, looking up at me and waiting for me to tell them all about my project, which I had labeled SEXUAL SENSATIONS, for the benefit of a cover-up label, I could see I had picked wisely and well.

Doreen Doremus, despite her lard and fat ass, could speak seven languages with that uncannily versatile tongue of hers.

Adele Ash was a six-foot honey-blonde from the wilds

41

of Milwaukee. A four-letter girl in the gymnastic departments of the university.

Corinne Murphy was a brunette with stacking like Liz Taylor and an inordinate amount of brains. She was a straight-A student in everything from thought to execution. Her fame preceded her frame.

Corinne Murphy liked the beehive hairdo for some reason but all the rest of her was the sort of stuff men buzz around constantly. Her measurements were 42-24-38.

Norma Davis and Alice Potter were almost look-alikes. Both medium pony chorus girl types, both blonde and vivacious and wickedly sexy in appearance; the kind of cute kids that make churchmen take a second look.

As for Pete Porter and Tony Eden, they were Joe College football types. Big, broad-shouldered, shaggy-haired Joe Namath copies with engaging grins as long as their equipment.

Quite a team. I was pleased with my perspicacity.

Doreen Doremus, hunched up on her tremendous buttocks at my very feet almost, looked up at me with adoring eyes. For a killing moment I thought she would forget we weren't alone and go into her routine. She always started by unzippering my fly from that position.

"Give, Professor," she chortled. "Sexual Sensations, huh? Sounds like a gas!"

Pete Porter and Tony Eden swapped sheepish grins. Like all big men, they came on gentle and poky and slow. But I wasn't fooled. Either of them could have snapped me in half like a breadstick. The girls, Corinne, Norma, Adele and Alice were all stunned into awesome silence. Being this close to Rod Damon in his own home, the place where he slept, was a little frightening. I could see some of them sneaking furtive looks toward the closed bedroom door. Maybe they thought I slept on a bed of nails. Or broads. I think they expected just about anything.

"Listen, kids," I began from the top. "I am about to do something daring. Even more daring than anything I ever attempted in Sexology. But it's necessary. And very important. The race is to the swift and all that jazz. I

42

don't know if any of you are that much interested in current events or who's sitting in the White House and what the moon shot is all about but it's high time you woke up to the fact that you are one hundred percent Americans. And what I am about to ask you to do has everything to do with God, Country—and believe it or not, Sex. Before I go a step further, anybody who doesn't want to do anything for the good old United States, he or she can leave the room right now. I can't have dissidents or rioters or flagburners in this crowd. So take a minute and think it over."

Contempt and anger ran around the room.

"I still got my draft card," Pete Porter said proudly.

"Who's a flagburner?" Tony Eden snapped peevishly.

The girls squealed out their patriotism and denials and Doreen Doremus waved everybody to silence, still looking up at me like a pixieish Buddha. Her tiny eyes were grinning.

"You running for election, Professor? Come on—quit this doubletalk. What do you want us to do?" This was greeted by that chorus of sounds and noises known as approval. The big boys settled down, still grumpily. They looked plenty burned up.

I assumed my most professorial air and let them have it. Without mentioning names or specifics, I told them all about Walrus-moustache's fears and the demand of my services and time and knowledge to help with the problem. Everybody, from six to sixty, has the James Bond fever, I guess. Nobody sees the ugly side, the killing, the betrayals, the double-dealing. They like it like it is in books and movies. Not one of my seven choices were troubled by any of that. As soon as I outlined my pitch and possible campaign, the room rang with enthusiasm and a babble of excitement and joy. You would have thought I had given them a month off from school with the man or woman of their choosing. It was amazing. I hadn't given out anything free at all.

"Gee," Doreen Doremus was aghast, for once. "From Russia with love——"

43

"Maybe," I said. "We're not sure. Remember it's our job to find out."

"Hey," Tony Eden snapped. "Do we get to carry guns with silencers on them?"

"And L-pills," Pete Porter chuckled. "I won't go any-place without my L-pills. They get me I won't talk—I'll take the pills."

"My," Corinne Murphy heaved her miracle forty-two chest, her eyes shining. "Mata Haris. Imagine."

Adele Ash jumped up and down, all six feet of her and all her assets jiggled and juggled pleasantly. She clapped her hands.

"Wow. We never had this in Milwaukee. Only beer and baseball!"

Norma Davis and Alice Potter, true to their resem-blance, were simply shaking their heads, their faces all awed and impressed. Like two little girls at the World's Fair. But their sullen sexy mouths were parted with some inner fire and lust for thrills. I know that type too. All sweetness and light but put a machine gun in their hands and they'd mow down F Troop. Or anybody else that got in their way.

I held up my hands. "Time, time. I'm glad you're all so keen, but this is not for kicks or a lark or anything you might want it to be. Spying is a nasty business. You could get killed. Very killed. So calm down, huh? And let's think constructively. Something has to be done and soon but I'd be the wrongest guy in the world if I let you all think this is a piece of cake. Like a party or something. Do you get that clear? You're risking your lives if you come into this with me. Now, ask all the questions you want. Now is the time."

They quieted down. And the classroom atmosphere I had instilled in them shot up. It was Tony Eden who got things going again.

"Do we carry guns?"

"No. No guns. It isn't necessary the way I intend to handle this operation. Next question."

"L-pills?" Pete Porter looked hopeful.

"No. Same reason. Next?"

44

"Gosh," Alice Potter murmured. "I've never been a spy before. Not ever. Do we have to learn codes and secret messages?"

I smiled. "Only what we set up among ourselves. We'll discuss that later. Well? Adele, Corinne, Norma—any questions?"

They shook their heads. Still awed, still almost frightened to death in that vicarious way that teenagers love. Doreen Doremus stirred. Her mouth was turned down in a sour mash.

"Yes, Fat A—er, Doreen?"

"Look, Professor. What is this all about? First you tell us you need spies and now you're cutting out all the fun and games. How can we operate as spies without the equipment?"

"That's a fair question, Doreen. I'll try to answer it."

"I mean—why did you pick me and the kids in the first place to help you?"

"I'll tell you if you'll shut up."

"Sorry." She blushed. "So tell us."

I looked them all in the faces and gave it to them straight. There was no other way. Anything less than the whole truth, and nothing but, would have been disastrous. A big mistake. They were my team now and I had to level with them.

"Okay. Here it is. I picked you seven swingers for very good reasons. Firstly, I'm fond of all of you. You've got brains and you're not afraid to experiment sexually. That says a lot for you. People who are like that have the ball in play and in control as far as I'm concerned. But now I'll tell you why you're the right people for the job. A—you're all only teenagers, still under twenty-one. B—you can all pass for hippies or what the experts call the dissident youth of this country. C—being young, you can move fast. Very fast. That may be important. D—to get our goal, accomplish this finding out about this heavy influx of spies, you may have to use your bodies. For Sex. Maybe wild, maybe highly experimental sex. I'm not sure yet but I know you can all do that too. Spies have one weakness; they will betray home, mother and their own

45

particular fatherland or motherland for a piece of ass. I'm counting on that. So you see, all in all, and putting all the points together, you're the best possible seven people for the job."

Doreen Doremus sniffed. "Huh. Why didn't you get that call girl from Puerto Rico in on this? Bet she can turn a trick or two."

"Down, catty. She has the Hong Kong Flu. Maybe later."

"And Clovis," Doreen sniffed some more. "You two were awfully palsy-walsy yesterday. Couldn't she join us?"

I laughed. "You see. The spy instinct comes naturally to you. Good. No. Clovis is confined to her room. Didn't you hear? She broke her leg this morning tripping in the hallway. Nothing serious but she is laid up. Damnedest accident."

"Yes, wasn't it?" Alice Potter laughed. "First time I ever saw a broken leg with hickey marks all over it." The rest of the girls snickered and jealous Doreen made a face. That girl absolutely adored me.

"Tripping in *bed,* you mean. Oh, why couldn't I be a size ten instead of an elephant!"

"Cheer up, Fat Ass," Corinne Murphy teased affectionately, "we all love you."

"Yeah," Pete Porter cracked, "there's a lot of you to love."

"Don't I know it!" Tony Eden boomed.

While they all got that laugh out of their systems, I pondered ruefully on the broken leg of Clovis Lee. The silly adorable dish had gotten a screwball notion at the eleventh hour of our fun. A running jump into the crotch of Damon. I had rolled over at that time to reach for a pillow. She had missed and wound up on the floor. A lousy way to end a memorable session in sexuality. But these things happen. Her leg would heal. She didn't break anything *really* important.

"Okay," I said when they had all stopped kidding Doreen. "So that's it. You are now Damon agents in your country's service. That means you keep your eyes and ears open. When you're out on dates, in the bars, the

46

theaters, the discotheques, the park—wherever you go, be on the lookout for strangers, suspicious-looking characters. Most especially anybody with a severe case of sunburn or windburn like I mentioned. You might even go over to some of the other colleges that are staging riots and sit-ins and see what you can find out. But above all, keep your lips sealed. Don't talk to anybody about this other than the people here now in this room. You report to me. I'll take it from there. Maybe we won't find out anything but I want us all to try."

Doreen smiled happily, her mind on the new game and forgetting what Mother Nature had done to her way back in the beginning.

"Gee, Professor, we ought to have a code or a signal. In case we do tumble to something or even get in trouble maybe. What about it, huh?" She was the real brains of the outfit, that one.

I thought about that a second. From the attitudes of the rest of them I saw that they agreed with her. After all, how could you be a secret agent without a code and passwords and things like that there?

"Check. Here's how we'll work it. When anyone of you wants to pass some information along and wants to get in touch with me—you will say: *'When the weather's hot and sticky that's no time to dunk the dicky, but when the frost is on the punkin' that's the time for dicky dunkin'!* Either say it or write it on a piece of paper. I don't subscribe to that proverb personally but that's immaterial. As for a trouble signal, a May Day—how about, *'There are sharks in these waters'*?"

"You said it," Tony Eden said feelingly, "that is a May Day if there ever was one." His hands slid meaningfully toward his own crotch. The girls didn't notice because he was standing behind them. Pete Porter winced. Expressively. Very well-hung men, the world over, share the same doubts and fears and anxieties. It isn't only me!

There wasn't much to talk about after that. All the girls were flushed and vicariously thrilled by their fresh emergence as Mata Haris. They were already exchanging the code signals and May Days back and forth the way the very young do when they immediately embrace a cause or a game. Or a joke. Tony Eden and Pete Porter gave me a little man-to-man buck-up talk and I let them. It was good for them to feel important and necessary, especially after the rough going-over their generation has gotten from all the expert media in the world: the newspapers, radio, TV and the assorted magazines with their articles and phony expert hooey. It must have been like a breath of fresh air for all of them to be needed and wanted the way I needed and wanted them. Without Dr. Joyce Brothers calling the shots.

So the whole thing went off without a hitch. They all understood what they had to do and they were agreeable. I was in charge—the women really like that—and everything was groovy, to hear them tell it. A gas. A ball. Spying was their bag now. You would have thought they'd been making the James Bond scene all their lives.

Contented, I let them return to their classes. I felt revivified myself. Also, I wanted to show Walrus-moustache I could handle a case without dashing off to remote corners of the world and sleeping with everybody. I could be the Master Spy in my own backyard.

After they had trooped out and I closed the door, I wasn't too surprised to find Doreen Doremus comfortably esconced in my bedroom, spread out on the counterpane with her arms behind her head, staring up at the ceiling. Her round moon face was set in angry circles.

"Fat Ass," I said kindly. It was my love call nickname for her. "You're jealous! You *really* are jealous. How *gauche!*"

"I am," she said in a faint little girl voice. "You tattooed that redheaded bitch Clovis all night, made a fast date with that Puerto Rican tramp and you never once let me come to you yesterday. You didn't even answer your phone!"

I sat down on the bed next to her. "I was busy. You heard. This whole operation—" She made room for me without batting an eye.

"Busy! Hah! Doing what—breaking Clovis Lee's right leg?"

"Fat Ass—"

She jerked erect, her mountainous folds and rolls of flesh shaking like jello. She flung her chubby arms around my neck and buried her really lovely face in my shoulder. Have you ever noticed how all the really fat girls have the damnedest beautiful faces?

"Oh, Roddy," she cooed. "I know I'm no bargain. I know you have so much to give that one woman will never be enough. Even one like me that's three women rolled in one. But the one in me that's aching to get out is all yours . . . you could at least have called me . . . I understand, you belong to the world, you have so much to give . . . but let me love you, snookums. Huh . . . please?"

"You can love me all you want if you promise not to call me snookums. Okay?"

"Why? You are my snookums, aren't you? You always will be. . . ."

"Suit yourself. But remember how important this job is. We have to find out about all those enemy agents infiltrating into this country. That comes first."

She giggled. "No, you always do. Time for our voice lesson." Slowly she had slid down the length of my body until she was curled up like a honey bear around an anthole. Her old familiar ploy and there wasn't a tongue from here to Africa that could match her. Like the great Swahili temptresses, the Arabian swabbers and the East Indian women who know all there is to know about the mouth and lips as oral delights, Fat Ass Doreen Doremus was in a class by herself. The most educated tongue in the universe. She didn't need the seventh method with me.

She was a virtuoso.

With her teeth, she ran my zipper down before she settled her own velvety talons of lip over the tentpole that flew out into her face, free from the confining trousers and jockey briefs.

"Fat Ass, I do like you. You know that. I admire your mind. I admire the fact that you speak seven tongues and didn't I ask you to come into this deal and . . . oh, don't do that. . . ."

"No?" she whispered softly, sure of herself, knowing

49

I was just talking. Her pink tongue, an incredible tool, had laved over every pore of me in a sliding, feathery ballet until now she was poised at the very tip of the matter.

"Fat Ass, that feels. . . ."

"Yes, Professor?"

Small, diametrically perfect little needles and pins of pleasure made me swell to the size of kings. I braced myself. Her next trick was always the killer, The one that did it.

"Mmmmmmm." I was reduced to a mere drooling idiot by that time.

"You were saying, Roddy?"

Her face touched me and then her tongue reached out to encircle. To love and destroy. I'm telling you. I advocate the straight sex act as the end-all in Sex, but the Doremuses of this world can make out some case for Frenching. When it is done masterfully, there is hardly anything you can compare it to. In or out of school.

"Go, Fat Ass, *go, go, go!*"

That shot out of me and it was as if I pressed a button in her head. She went down, bit, and the world was a big noisy roar of flooding cataracts, exploding skyrockets and jet bombers colliding. The room did the frug and every living inch of me was bathed in the bursting radiance of a golden shower. I fell back on the bed, literally helpless, and she didn't let go, mashing her great weight to me, her mouth vised onto the biggest thing about me. What a mouth. At turns velvety and smooth, at others, biting, exploring, roving, maddeningly active and expert. For a long interval, all the care, worry and trouble in my mucked-up life fled from me. Leaving with every drop of volatile dew sucked from me by the amazing student known as Doreen Doremus, Fat Ass to the world of the university.

Rita Cortez had made me cross over the bridge about four times in a different method of extraction. But Doreen Doremus had managed the same thing with a direct contact. With lip service. It is a goofy hemisphere all around.

Later on, when we had both come up for air, Doreen and I talked about it. I held her in my arms on the bed and she wept softly into my neck. Wept—she blubbered.

"Oh, Roddy, why are you so big and why do I have to be built so small down there?"

"Que sera, sera."

"It isn't fair. I ought to get an operation, make myself big enough. I got to ball you, Roddy. At least once."

"Don't be ridiculous. You're fine just the way you are. You know I'm a freak too. Nobody's as big as I am. You'll see. Someday you'll meet Mr. Right."

"Wrong," she said vehemently. "All I gotta do is lose about two hundred pounds and get down to a svelte one fifty and you'll see how I wear you out." Angrily, but with great affection, she slapped at it and it swung back toward her like a homing pigeon.

"Cut that out."

"You mean literally? I think I'd need a cleaver—"

"Funny girl. Listen, you pay attention to what I told the rest of the kids. This is no picnic. Be careful. And just learn whatever you can."

"Ahhh—" She slipped from my arms and roamed down to my waist again. "We'll do just fine. Wait and see."

"Hey—where are you going?"

"To Buckingham Palace to see the Queen," she growled. "Where the hell do you think I'm going?"

"Just asking. You don't have to bite my head off."

"Now there's an idea——"

Me and my big mouth. Her and her wild one. I had to close my eyes and hang onto her shoulders as she downed tools and really did me up brown. I don't know how she did it but she did it. Every time. The room tilted again and my insides cannonaded with ecstasy.

Windburn, sunburn, ice burn, hell.

I got a lipburn all the way to the floor.

Later, much later, as flagged out as I was and I mean flagged because Old Glory was like it looks fluttering in a stiff breeze, I remembered I was Walrus-moustache's man. A spy chief. A head, as it were. Before I packed

51

Doreen Doremus back to her dormitory room, I had a brief confab with her. I didn't know *that* much about her. I had never really asked, the way you usually do with people you are very intimate with.

"Fat Ass, fill me in."

"Again? Didn't you have enough, piggy?"

"Quit clowning. Everybody knows you speak seven languages. But I'll bet nobody really knows what the seven are."

"I speak English," she laughed, wrestling into a bra that would have accommodated three women. She had breasts as large as basketballs. And they bounced just as much too.

"I know you speak French," I said acidly. "Like an expert. Now what else is there? Stop clowning. It may be important."

"Isn't everything?" she sighed. "You men."

"Give."

She counted on her pudgy fingers. "English, French, German, Russian, Cantonese, Italian and Yiddish."

"Yiddish?" I frowned. "And I thought you said seven—?"

"Isn't English a language, Rod?" She giggled. "I know it sounds like seven others besides English but you got to admit it's more impressive that way."

"Sure. Yiddish and *not* Hebrew?"

"A little of that, of course, but they're two different lingos, really."

"They sure are, *shiksa*."

"Look at the *shegetz* calling the kettle black! Besides, it's like the man said—when you're in love the whole world is Jewish."

I saw her to the door. She got another fine stranglehold on my neck and pushed her three hundred and fifty pounds at me. I felt like I was waltzing with a hippo. But she was a good kid. She was always a good kid. I had used her and I could use her again. For something else besides French lessons. She was really the sharpest of the seven knives I had enlisted in the services of the Thaddeus X. Coxe Foundation.

She pushed back after biting my ear. Her eyes were gleaming like Romeo and Juliet. What a character.

"Like me, Roddy?"

"Yes, I do, surprisingly. A lot."

"Then you stay away from Clovis, bad leg and all. And that call girl with the oh so white skin. Want me to scratch her eyes out? I could, you know. I'm the type."

"Better not. She'd scratch back. She's just the type. A hellcat, I'll wager."

Doreen snorted.

"She's just plain pussy to me. With eyes on my man. I fight for my man."

"Please, Fat Ass. Stop reading those romantic novels and seeing old foreign movies on TV. Nobody talks that way, anymore."

"No?" she sneered. "I do."

"Forget it. Go get some beauty sleep now. You need it."

It was the wrong thing to say. And I didn't mean it like it sounded. She gave a small gasp of pain as if I had stuck a knife in her and then turned and barreled out of the door. She was gone down the hallway in a trailing cloud of mini-skirt, scarf and perfume before I could stop her.

Resignedly, I began to close the door.

But I didn't get it shut fast enough. Clovis Lee loomed in my eyes. Tall, willowlike Clovis, as firm and energetic as ever, despite the swaths of bandages and cast making her right leg a stiff thing to walk on. She was leaning on a cane, with nothing but a filmy Baby Doll to cover her and she was all out of breath. Small wonder. She had to come down three floors to get to my rooms. And she must have come from the other direction for Doreen Doremus not to have seen her. She hobbled into the room before I could stop her. I got the door shut in a hurry. Her fanny glistened almost nakedly through a sheer silk gown.

"What the hell are you doing here?" I rasped. "You should be in bed."

"My notion exactly," she sighed, trembling like a school-

53

girl. "I need your hot water bottle again. Bad. I told you I was wanton."

Wanton.

And wanting.

Ah, these poor girls. One taste of Damon and they lose all their inhibitions, proprieties and marbles. It figured.

"Come on in," I said, "the water's fine."

So the Great Spy Hunt was delayed another evening. What the hell. Rome wasn't built in a day. There was always time. The great Italian lover Marcello Dambrosino always tipped his manicured fingers to that slogan. Always time for a roll in the hayrick.

Dambrosino is the man who lived to the ripe old age of ninety-nine, after seventeen marriages and forty-seven children and the only reason he ever stopped making love is that he went the way all Great Lovers want to go. Shot to death climbing out the bedroom window with his pants down, leaving a weeping best friend's wife behind him. And a lot of other men's wives to mourn his passing. I hear the funeral in Salerno was the biggest thing since Sophia came out of the hills to be a movie star.

Everything is velvet in the Sex world.

That night I learned how to make love to a woman with her right leg in a plaster cast. The cane was a great prop, too.

Aside from very, very *carefully,* we found a few new positions to add to my constantly increasing lore on the subject. Clovis Lee was a happy, willing participant. So eager for knowledge. So hungry for love games. And not too darn particular about winning all the time, either.

Me?

Big Spy Chief or not, I was in clover.

In Clovis, too.

CHAPTER FIVE

A week passed.

Mission Secret Agent began to look like *Mission: Impossible*. Oh, the kids tried. How they tried. In between attending classes, doing their usual school thing at the

54

university, they went after the assignment I had given them tooth and nail. And muscles and panties, too. I was simply astounded how they got into the spirit of the thing.

Pete Porter and Tony Eden staked out one of the hottest discotheque clubs in town because they found out it was run by a tall, dark-haired Russian doll known as Madame Russky. So they applied the pressure and the hot technique they had learned in my classes. What it all added up to was that both were invited up to Madame Russky's bedroom, both came back to me with silly expressions on their faces, and it was a red herring from top to bottom. The Madame was an Irish girl from Brooklyn out to turn a fast buck by giving her dive some atmosphere. So all Porter and Eden got out of that was some jumps into the bedroom. And an advanced education into the ways and mores of female hustlers. The Madame charged them fifty bucks apiece and when they were unable to pay the bill, both of them had to fight their way out of the place past an army of bouncers with broken bottles, blue-black jaws and lousy manners. So much for that.

Adele Ash had a brainwave.

She went down to the local bus stop which pours people into town from about four different cities and wound up picking up every strange-looking guy she saw. With her sexy equipment, it wasn't hard. She was also a six-footer who could take care of herself. But after seven days of making love to every suntanned man who got off the bus, even she was pooped out. Sore but satisfied. But no spies did she catch.

The week droned on, full of no surprises, lots of activity and absolutely no headway.

Corinne Murphy, what with her forty-two's showing in tight blouse, mini-skirt and rouged up like Singapore Sal, got herself arrested on the corner of Twelfth and Main for loitering for purposes of prostitution. Poor kid. The cops propositioned her on the way to jail in the squad car so she got off for good behavior. When she told me about it, she had a happy look on her face. It seems like one of the arresting officers was almost as big as I am. That sort of loused up Corinne for the week. She dated

55

that particular cop every night that week but she swore she would like 'keep her eyes open' while she traveled in police circles.

Norma Davis and Alice Potter, being such peas in a pod, decided to make it work for them. So they worked together. And all that got them was a gang bang job in Ferry Park by a whooping bunch of college boys from the other side of town. Nobody was confused by the resemblance. La Davis got screwed just as many times as La Potter did. And all these two ladies could tell me was that it seemed like everybody in the world had a great suntan. Or windburn or whatever the hell we were looking for. My plans weren't exactly paying fruit. Or bearing it, either.

Doreen Doremus tried the hardest, bless her. She rigged herself up to look like a sad, fat little French doll who sopped up gallons of beer in all the bars in town. She tried about fifteen of them in one night. All she got for her pains was a whopping hangover, sick tummy and a promise to herself that she would never drink beer again. But she did manage to draw up a list of suspects for me. From all the bars and all the men, she had found something like seventeen suspicious-looking characters, all with browned skins and funny accents. She'd gotten too stewed to identify the accents but she had made seventeen dates for later on in the week. When the time came to check them out, I went with her as an irate husband routine whose wife had been insulted. All seventeen of the jokers turned out to be the usual sad lot: straying husbands, perverts, lonely guys and single bums out for a couple of laughs with a very very fat girl. The whole project wound up a big round zero. My big plan looked all shot.

The kids were game and willing but you don't become a spy overnight, I guess. Even James Bond must have had to take lessons. And Mata Hari. As good as she was, look what happened to her. They shot her in front of a firing squad. I was getting kind of leery about the whole mess.

Meanwhile, I followed my own natural bent.

With the university library at my disposal as well as all the other goodies, I boned up on Alaska, the Arctic,

56

the North Pole and outer Siberia. Particularly on the subject of the exposure of the skin to such climates. I learned plenty. The kind of skin burn I had seen on the cats in Walrus-moustache's film had exactly that sort of color. I was convinced of that as I was that L'il Abner lives in Dogpatch. It was still my greatest clue. And only lead. All that time, reports came filtering into my life from Walrus-moustache. Piped by phone, message and data sheets. All in code. But all of those added up to one thing. Spies, spies and more spies were being picked up all over the country. The total was swelling. The proper agencies were leaving a lot of them untouched, hoping they would lead to a big killing. But with all of that, Walrus-moustache was in a tizzy. The problem was getting bigger and in a full week I hadn't accomplished much of anything.

Except to watch seven kids make eager, willing fools of themselves. They'd get better, of course, but right now they were the rankest kind of amateurs. I was feeling like a butcher sending lambs to the slaughterhouse. Or the little old Judas goat, which is the same thing.

University days and nights had to go on, however.

Miss Rita Cortez was still incapacitated with the Hong Kong Flu so I spent my evenings nursing Clovis Lee back to health. She was a very slow healer. And she was playing her cards just right. Who could boot such a darling gorgeous redhead out into the cold? I couldn't. Besides, she helped keep the rest of the girls off my back. Doreen Doremus was far too busy being a *femme fatale* in the spy department to notice. Anyhow I was able to keep them both on the hook without either of them knowing it. Or at least, so I thought. You can never be sure about dames.

On the tenth day, Walrus-moustache lost his patience. He called me late in the evening while I was in bed with Clovis Lee. I had been showing her only the Japanese method all night. It's very interesting in that it allows for complete absorption of the female with the male. He could be peeling a grape while his Lotus-Blossom is making with the sexual play. So I easily answered the phone while Clovis, without stopping, bless her red hair and fine persistence, continued to inundate my body with kisses. I

57

stared over the wonderful coastline of her buttocks as she bent to me and kept the phone out of her way. She was busily and lustily manipulating me between her two palms with a halt every now and then to softly kiss me in *extremis*. Her plaster cast leg was not in the way at all.

"Damon," Walrus-moustache snarled into the transmitter. "We are simply not getting anywhere!"

"Says you."

"Ten days since I passed you the ball and it remains in your back court. Really, old man, I expected something by this time. Not even a dribble of news?"

Clovis was slurping noisily but he couldn't hear her.

"Not a drop," I said, "but my team is functioning on all six. Er—seven."

"You did say *functioning?*" I could hear his eternal sigh. "My dear colleague, if you have avoided flying to parts unknown again solely in order to arrange another of your wild sex sprees, I shall never forgive you. I mean that, Damon."

"Stop beating your gums. Listen to this—" I gave him a rundown on the zeal and ambition of Doreen and Corinne and Norma and Alice and Adele and Pete and Tony. He listened. While it was true all of the report was negative, he saw some glimmer of hope in such efforts.

"Well—" he sounded mollified. "Perhaps I was a bit hasty."

"Perhaps you were. But while you're on the phone— do you have anything for me?" On that last, Clovis had gotten a generous swallow going and I moaned with pleasure. Walrus-moustache exploded.

"Damn you, Damon! You're in bed with a woman right now! Even as the world hangs in the balance! I knew it!"

I blew my top. "What did you expect me to be in bed with, a Rhesus monkey? Stop lecturing me, will you? Give me information instead. Has anything new developed? Don't worry about my sex life so much—are you queer or something?"

I didn't have to see him to know that he was gritting his teeth and hanging onto his control with all he had.

When his voice came back over the wire, it was ginger-peachy sweet.

"No, nothing outstanding has happened. It's just that we keep rounding up batches and batches of spies who are dropping into this country like flies. I just had Spokane on the wire. The very latest in enemy agents was picked up last night by the immigration people. Another of your peculiarly windburned men. They seem to drop out of the blue, you know and if you could find the time to forget about your sexual hungers—well, we would appreciate that, dear Mr. Damon. After all, the Coxe Foundation does make all your many pleasures possible, doesn't it?"

I sat up quickly and Clovis gulped for air. I waved her off and stared at the phone. A hot flash, other than Clovis' brand, had soared through my head.

"Cut the crap," I said. "Did you say Spokane? Spokane, Washington?"

"Congratulations," he said drily. "You're up on your geography also, it seems."

"I'm always up, you walrus-faced bastard and if you don't stop needling me, I'll resign right now. Listen. I've got an idea—"

"Such as?"

"Such as you call those immigration people, tell them to hold Ivan whatever his name is for me and I'll catch a plane there in the morning to talk to them and him."

"It's useless, Damon." We were talking business now so his manner softened. "He has been mute and veritably catatonic since they caught him. Not so much as a word. Since we don't torture people, what can you hope to accomplish?"

"That's my lookout. I'll be bringing one of my ladies with me. Doreen Doremus. You can register her as my translator, okay? But get me two plane tickets on a morning flight. Okay?"

"Well—it's gratifying to hear you sounding like an agent instead of a cockhound. I don't know what you're up but if you can get anything out of that man, it will be worth it. Wait just a second." I drummed the phone while he was gone and Clovis quietly went back to her

59

homework. A completely unruffled female at all times. She had turned her back to me again and neatly glided me into the wondrous caverns of her thighs. She found the darkest, most inviting recess and let me roost there. I began to push up and down. She sighed. And pushed back. We had a nice thing going when Walrus-moustache got back on the line.

"Very well. It's done. Flight 19 tomorrow morning at ten fifteen. American Airlines. Do be on time. Reservations for two and if you turn this into another of your sexual jaunts, you shall pay, Damon. Not only in dollars and cents. Understood?"

I stuck my tongue out at the phone. *"Nah, hah, nah!"* I razzed and hung up.

Clovis Lee paused to peer back at me over one shapely shoulder. Her falling red hair hung like a mantle down her back.

"What was that all about, Rod . . . ?"

"Shut up," I commanded, "and screw."

Laughing happily, she raised her splendid body so that her fine torso hung freely and her really excellent buttocks filled my eyes. I slid just as happily beneath her and she raised herself to her knees. It was the vastly underrated Blind Spot ploy where you come at the target from below and drive upward while the target accepts the challenge and fights you back by pushing downwards. It's a gorgeous arrangement all around and both sides come out ahead, no matter how you look at it. A super scuttle in any man's league.

Clovis Lee had a lot of very nice habits, not the least of which was her utter abandon and willingness to do what the doctor ordered. In this case, me being the doctor, of course. When her bad leg got better, I fully intended her to join my spy team. She could be very useful. I was sure of that.

By the time we were both primed and well-oiled and hanging in there was a slippery gambit, I reversed her so that we were both once more facing each other. She never seemed to tire although her blues singer voice always had that catchy out-of-breath quality which was one of

60

the simple little things that made her such a sexy number.

I hung her on me once more and her marvelous mammaries spread out across my chest warming me. She wriggled her toes. The wriggling only made me slide deeper and deeper into the greatest snake pit of them all. If the loonies could see those kind of pits, they'd never go out of their minds at all. It might drive them back *into* their minds. Sex can be a great healer, when properly applied.

"Rod?"

"I can't escape from you."

"Do me a favor?"

"At your service, Clovis."

"Can we try that seventh method again? You know what Rita Cortez did to you and we started last week—I think I got the hang of it now and I would like to try a few things———"

"*Apres vous,* lady. And let's get this show on the road!"

"Ohhhhh," she whimpered. "I'm so glad. You'll be leaving town tomorrow and I would like to give you something to remember me by. Let me do you first." She scampered off me and dragged me by the hands to the center of the room. The thick carpet beneath our feet felt like whipped cream now.

"I won't have any trouble remembering you," I declared. "After all, how many females with a broken leg do you think I've slept with? You're my very first."

"Honest?" She had paused, thrilled.

"I'll swear it on a pile of Plaster of Paris."

"Oh, you—" she said, pushing me playfully across the chest.

I pushed her back. Again, without using my hands. She gave a girlish little laugh, the smile left her face, she got deadly serious and then she came toward me. Circling, taking my measure, watching every line of my body. When she got to the main line, she stopped and targeted in on me. Mouth first.

I closed my eyes.

You don't need airplanes to fly, all the time.

Spokane was on the morning agenda and Doreen Doremus would wing with me toward the non-talking spy but that night with Clovis Lee I touched all the clouds there are. One to Nine inclusive.

We didn't do much talking, either.

We didn't have to.

Action still speaks louder than words.

CHAPTER SIX

The confrontation with the spy who came in from the cold (I *thought*, thanks to the severe reddish-tan wind-burn) was something for the books. This cat was the original no-spikka-da-English prize from way back. Walrus-moustache had pulled out all the stops. Doreen Doremus, tickled down to her·fat toes, boarded a special jet with me out of our university town and in three short hours we were in Spokane. A special car met us at the fly-field and we got driven over to the immigration building in two shakes of a Fed's tail. Then it was really red carpet all the way. We got ushered into a private room in a maze of cubicles and doors and corridors and were left alone with the prisoner. A bald-headed guy named Perkins with a blue suit and white tie told me we could interrogate our man as long as we liked. I didn't have the foggiest idea just how long that would be. He looked about as talkative as a clam.

Doreen, of course, was in her glory. On leave from class, out with dear darling Damon and all alone with a real spy-type important operation. Naturally, she couldn't keep her hands off me. Both on the plane and in the private car from the field. I had to forcibly tell her that our personal love life would have to wait until we interviewed the prisoner. She just giggled and hugged me and fiddled all over the lot until I slapped her hands. When she finally gave up she had left a good thirty-two-teeth hickey on my left thigh. Cute kid. But as soon as we were alone with the spy, she settled down and was all business the way I wanted her to be. After all, wasn't the future of America at stake? Her tongue would just have to stand in line, that's all.

The spy-type was sitting in a wooden chair behind a wooden table in a plain, no-furniture room without windows. Which was all right with me. I hadn't come to socialize with him. Doreen fidgeted a little, all her great bulk unhappy about no chairs but she took it with a stiff upper hip and hovered behind me.

I studied the gaunt fish the immigration boys had hauled in. He was skinny, all right. About five nine in height but real wire-thin and strong-looking in spite of that. Also, he was a blue-eyed blond. Which made that damn bronzed-blue coloring of his more unique than ever.

I led off with my right.

"What's your name?"

He shrugged. His eyes flickered over me and then over Doreen. His expression was almost contemptuous.

"How did you get into this country?"

Again he shrugged.

"Who sent you to the United States?"

He spread his hands and shifted in his chair. As silent as the Sphinx.

"Come on. We know who your friends are. Quit stalling! It will go hard for you if you don't talk."

Every cliché police station line in the book I threw at him. For about a half hour. He didn't let out so much as a yawn. Though I could see he felt like yawning. Doreen fidgeted some more. I was getting restless myself. Also, my voice was beginning to sound like a broken LP.

"You bastard," I muttered. "Would you believe I'd dearly love to kick your ass all over this room and I just may do that just for the hell of it?"

Now, he smiled and spoke. In perfect unbroken English marred only by a soft Latin slur, he said, "I stand on my constitutional rights as a human being. You will not strike me, sir. If you do, I shall have your shield. Or whatever they give you sort of people. I have nothing further to say. You are wasting your time."

"I sure am," I admitted, feeling defeated. "You won't talk at all, huh?"

"My lips are as they say, sealed."

"Where did you get that windburn? North Pole? Been on a long sea voyage in the Aleutian Islands maybe?"

"No comment."

"You said it. All right. You can't smoke and you don't get a drink of water until you open up. Don't go away." Turning around I took Doreen by the arm and led her to a far corner of the barren room. She looked surprised until I whispered in her ear.

"Listen, we have to trick this bastard. He's too smart. So you wait until I start in on him again. Same barrage of questions. After about five minutes, I want you to order him to *Stand Up*. In *Russian* first. Then if nothing happens wait awhile longer and then try Chinese. And then maybe German or Spanish. You dig? These birds are trained to obey. Maybe force of habit will give us the lead we want. We got to crack him or this whole trip is a frost and Walrus-moustache will scream about me wasting money."

"Walrus who?"

"Never mind. Come on now. Do like I told you. The next play is yours."

We broke it up and got back to the interrogation table. The gaunt, blue-eyed blond man was almost smiling. As if we were planning some kind of trick and it would be a cold day in hell—or wherever he came from—before we could out-fox him. Doreen kept a straight chubby face and folded her arms. She looked like Two-Ton Tessie doing that bit. The spy didn't wrinkle his forehead but looked up at me coolly.

So I started all over again. Same routine. Same rapid-fire series of stock questions. All the ones I knew he wouldn't answer. He didn't and I was getting hoarse again when Doreen suddenly barked in what must have been Russian, something that sounded like a double order of beef stroganoff. But all she got for that was a curious look from the spy. So he did another of his shrugs and blinked his eyes sleepily like he was tired. I hid my disappointment and groaned inwardly. But I kept on pumping him, never letting up for a second. He had all to do to keep

64

track of all the queries. Even though he had the standard *"No comment"* or a wag of the head to reply with.

Just as I was all set to think I was going to go through the rest of my life sounding like Mr. Green the Frog, Doreen cut loose with another burst of words. I don't speak Chinese, Cantonese or Mandarin or any of the hundred dialects they have but I know a crisp order of chop suey when I hear it.

So did the gaunt man.

Because he jumped to his feet, snapped to attention, drew himself up proudly and only when he realized he had been tricked, did he grin sheepishly and slide back down to his seat like a sullen schoolboy. Doreen laughed out loud and I smiled, too. We had hit the jackpot.

"Well, well, well. So you don't send your laundry out, eh? That's nice to know. You speak Chinese. Red Chinese, perchance? Do tell us, pal."

He glowered and said nothing. But small beads of perspiration began to finely gather on his forehead.

"Come on, you're no Oriental. But you savvy Chinee. How come? Pretty unusual for an Occidental, isn't it? Or are you the illegitimate son of a teahouse girl? Live in Shanghai, maybe? Get your mail from Peking?"

Again, no answer. But he was squirming on the hook. I gave Doreen the high-sign again. She was really enjoying herself now. Also she had obviously been doing a little mental arithmetic. The man's coloring and all. The next *Stand Up* command she fired from my left side was in plain old musical Spanish. A romance language which when not spoken too fast is a lovely Castilian sound.

Our spy nearly jumped a foot in the air. When he came down, he was really sweating now. Like a stuck pig or a spy caught flatfooted.

"Si, si, si," I laughed. "And a couple of *olés* to you, too. Now. It's all finally becoming quite clear to me. You'd better start spilling, man, or it's the hot seat for you. We still fry spies in this backwards country of ours and now that we can guess that you're very probably a Latin of some kind who speaks Chinese besides Spanish, wouldn't you say we were getting warmer?"

65

"I would," Doreen chortled. "Let's hand him over to the electric chair committee."

He didn't know about things like that but he got the gist of the idea. His hands started to drum nervously on the table. He looked at me and a weak smile barely lit up his face. His teeth were slightly yellowish, spoiling a fairly attractive appearance.

"Good idea," I said. "After all, he's a spy. We got half of what we want. We'll pick up some more of his friends and that'll be the end of it. Come on, Doreen. Let's go." We turned to leave and he didn't disappoint me.

"Wait, *amigo!*" he cried.

I turned. "Something you wanted to say, mister?"

"Yes—I—please. You must not kill me. I will never see Rosita again. I could not bear that."

"I guess Rosita couldn't either. Your wife?"

"Wife?" He winced. "She is my mistress. My sweetheart, my life. I won't let you kill me for this political life I lead—"

"Do tell us more. And don't spare me the details about that suntan of yours, *amigo*. I'm more interested in how you got that than anything else. Believe me."

"Very well." He drew himself up stiffly. "I would die for *amor* but not for politics. This electric chair—you will save me from it if I tell you what you wish to know?"

"You have the word of a Coxeman."

He didn't know what that was but it must have sounded as impressive to him as the electric chair had. He began to talk. I listened and Doreen Doremus made notes. With squeals of genuine pleasure.

After about fifteen minutes, we had all the facts we needed. I began to feel like a very clever fellow indeed. Almost a super-agent. Baldheaded Perkins was as awed with my success with the former-clam of a prisoner as anyone. As the prisoner was led away, Perkins collared me.

"How did you do it?" he asked, his eyes popping.

"Simple. I threatened to cut off his wang and drop him by parachute into the first nudist colony I saw."

"But, but, but—that's *unethical*. That's—ridiculous!"

66

"Sure it is. But my secrets are my own. Toodle-oodle, Perkins. Don't pick up any more wooden spies."

With that, Doreen Doremus and I took our leave. I had enough facts and figures to satisfy even Walrus-mous-tache's greatest hunger for information. I was feeling pretty cocky, I guess. A fact which Doreen noticed on the ride back to the airport. We were flying right back to the university, and she was warming me under the lap robes in the car.

"Will what we learned really help, Roddy?"

"You bet your ass it will. We got the pipeline now. We know how they do it. Once my friends and the proper authorities know, they can bring this spy traffic to a roaring halt."

"I'm proud of you, Professor."

"A lot of the credit is yours, Doreen. I never would have swung it without the Chinese and Spanish words. Good girl."

"If you mean that, then give me my reward."

"What, right here?"

"No, silly, back at the university. Let me spend the night with you. I'm lonely for you, *boobelah*. And hungry."

"I can refuse you nothing. It's a deal."

That made her so damn happy and grateful she nearly squeezed the family jewels into a mess of jelly. I cried out and she stopped just in time. The poor girl didn't know her own strength.

On the big, shining jet winging back to home base, I wrote out my report to Walrus-moustache, transcribed from Doreen Doremus' notes. Looking back, at the time it seemed to me like I had wrapped the whole assignment up very nicely. My prisoner at Immigration had talked his head off because he didn't want to leave life without loving his Rosita again and I figured he had told the truth. He had, all right, but what I didn't understand was that the problem was really just beginning. I didn't know that I had merely opened a Pandora's box, a different kind for me admittedly, and the whole world was getting ready to tumble down around my ears.

Anyhow, the report when decoded would read:

IMMIGRATION PRISONER WAS A NATIVE CUBAN WHO SPEAKS CHINESE AS WELL AS SPANISH. RED CHINESE ARE SETTING UP A NETWORK IN OCCIDENTAL U.S.A. WITH SUCH TYPES. A BLUE-EYED BLOND WHO WOULD NEVER BE TAKEN FOR ORIENTAL. WINDBURN EXPLANATION: THESE MEN ARE TRAINED IN CHINA AND MUST ENTER COUNTRY THROUGH ALASKA. RUSSIA, SPARSELY POPULATED IN SIBERIA MUST HAVE TOO FEW PATROLS ON THE COAST. AGENTS COME UP TO THE BERING STRAIT, MOTOR BOAT ACROSS THE 21 MILES TO COAST THEN WORK THEIR WAY DOWN. ALONG ROUTE, THEY GET WINDBURNED, SUNBURNED, ETC. CLEAR?

I TOLD YOU THIS TRIP WAS NECESSARY NOW YOU CARRY THE BALL. I'VE GOT MY CLASSES TO KEEP ME BUSY.

DAMON

I was smug when I finished that report. Spokane had been my Appamattox Courthouse I thought and I was General Grant coming back with the other guy's sword. Oh, yeah.

Doreen Doremus was snoozing in the plane seat next to me, her gigantic proportions crushing me. But I didn't care. I had delivered the bacon, hadn't I? And I could sort of ease up on spying and go back to what I do best, making love to willing women. And getting paid for it.

We hit some bumpy weather over Wyoming, thunderheads racing ahead of us, shaking up the plane and making Doreen stir her fat ass uncomfortably. I didn't pay any attention to that. I should have. It was an omen of the worst kind.

I was heading down the chute to doom and I didn't even have an inkling. Man, we really all are a bunch of

68

the worst kind of saps sometimes. Especially when we don't even stop to read the handwriting on the wall.

The prisoner had talked.

I had listened.

And I thought that was that.

It was, all right, but there was a helluva lot more to come. Everything the prisoner left out. That he couldn't tell me. That he didn't know. But how was I to guess? I'm no spy. Not really.

So, bad weather to one side, I slept the rest of the flight in. With Doreen Doremus at my side and a song in my heart.

My muscles felt pretty good too.

I was feeling my oats and could have taken on the entire chorus of a big Broadway musical. Or the full enrollment complement at the university. I had the world by the balls.

After all, me and James Bond, we were men among men. With or without silencer-pistols. And I'd done my little bit without even firing a shot. In anger or anything else.

So I slept.

While the world went smash. The one I had built so very nicely and carefully at the university. The world I loved in so happily.

Red China is many thousands of miles away from the United States, but just like the headlines and TV news specials have been showing us for years, it can be as close as the girl next door sometimes. Or a very bad case of halitosis or B.O.

Or the corpse.

Stick around and I'll give you the gory details.

It isn't pretty.

Not a bit of it.

In fact it's messier than a Chicago slaughterhouse during business hours. And you know how badly those places can smell in the foul old summertime.

It makes you want to buy out all the clothespins there are on the market.

To get the stink of death out of your nose.

69

CHAPTER SEVEN

The dream of peace and serenity continued for about two weeks. My team of seven secret service boys and girls had kept busy despite my injunction to lay off. But hell, they liked the fun and games so well, they kept up the pace. It turned out that big and handsome Tony Eden was acey-deucy and was carrying on his investigations in the gay sections of the city where boys will be girls and vice versa. I didn't find that out until Doreen Doremus reported that big Tony was shacked up with one of the most notorious homos in the books. Well, he wasn't the first very outwardly masculine guy who liked to swing both ways. The woods are full of them. I myself let the gang have their fun and went back to my research and women, in equal parts. Walrus-moustache had been pleased as a dog who just got laid with my report. He sort of dropped out of my life again. Clovis Lee's leg healed, but she continued her private studies with me, and Doreen managed to get her licks in, too. Rita Cortez was finally on the mend and I had her filed in the back of my mind for a future engagement. I could wait. She wasn't going anyplace and she had signed up for the whole course. The rest of my lady spies took the *Sexual Sensations* cover title quite seriously. The Misses Ash, Murphy, Davis and Potter kept on beating the bushes for strange-looking men with windburns. Unfortunately they found a barrelful of them. Meanwhile they got their kicks again, and I didn't think a thing about it until Walrus-moustache called me on the phone again one dark Friday night.

"Mexico," he said, without preamble.

"Sure," I laughed. "It's a great place to visit but I wouldn't want to live there."

"You don't understand," he moaned unhappily. "Your Spokane trip was very successful. We learned about the Bering Strait pipeline and we put a stop to it. But now they're coming up through Mexico. Hordes of windburned men! Only this time they are genuine sunburns. Mexico is rather torrid, you know."

70

"Oh, no," this time I groaned. "Not again!"

"Afraid so, Damon. Sorry. You'll have to keep your team in the field. And your eyes and ears open. This is a direct order. Do what you can."

"But I'm in the midst of a great research idea. I haven't got the time. Did you know that a naked woman, properly stimulated, will do just about anything to be satisfied? Take the case of that ninety-year-old woman who was accidentally ingested with Spanish fly. She took this big gilded candelabra—"

"Damon, spare me. This still has top priority in your case. Don't let the Coxe Foundation down, old boy."

"Have I ever?" I snarled. "I've done plenty for you birds. I'm not made of stone, you know."

"You certainly are not. Goodbye and keep in touch."

When he hung up I felt like breaking all my *Carmen* records, tearing up my bullfighter posters and cursing Ricardo Montalban in all seven of Doreen Doremus' languages. Mexico! Take it away!

Now I knew I would have to enlist Rita Cortez's aid. Maybe she was Puerto Rican but she was bound to know more about Mexico than Brooklyn. Or Spokane. Or Boston.

So the big Spy Hunt was still on. All I had won was a breather for myself. Now I was glad the kids were still doing their homework. At least, I hadn't called them off the case, so they wouldn't have to start all over again. But it was tough on me. I *was* in the middle of the research project I had mentioned to Walrus-moustache and already I had lined up three topflight students of 36-22-36 proportions and one hundred precent willingness to co-operate. The program was set for Monday night. That was only three days off. I didn't want anything to interrupt my scheduling or my plans. Damn the Coxe Foundation anyway. What made them think I was such a great spy?

Somebody had latched onto the leak about Spokane and the traffic in windburned men had stopped. Now it seemed to be that Mexico was the back door to the United States. How? Why?

Those were questions I had the order to find the answers

to and I didn't like it a bit. But Walrus-moustache and his Coxemen called the tune and I would have to dance. It didn't matter that I wasn't Astaire or Kelly in that department.

Glumly, grimly, my whole dream of peaceful coexistence with my coeds shot to hell and back, I put my research project aside for another day.

It was just about that time that the shit really hit the fan. And the mess that followed wasn't going to be easy to clean up. I'm not much good with a broom, either.

Doreen Doremus had a hot tip. She wanted to follow it down. She told me all about it late that night as we wound up a licking session in fine fettle. Doreen hadn't lost her touch. If anything, she was better than ever. As I lay back, relaxing, and she squatted nakedly alongside me, still playing with me, her little eyes were snapping with enthusiasm.

"You see, Roddy? That office building with the travel agency sign in it—what with all those guys coming in and out—hell, they all can't want to travel at this time of year. It just isn't kosher. I'll bet the joint is a front of some kind."

"Maybe. Aren't you tired of being Fat Ass, Girl Spy?"

"I'm just tired of being Fat Ass. Oh, I don't mind when you call me that. You say it *different* . . . you know what I mean?"

There was a bottle of Johnny Walker Black Label. We had been sipping from it steadily. I had the blues, I guess, along with the hots. And Doreen had been a great palliative for both. It was a helluva night to be morose.

"Want another drink, Fat Ass?"

"Yes. I'll share anything with you, Lover."

"You're a screwball," I said.

"I'm a woman in love," she said proudly. "I'm not ashamed of it. You should be glad."

"There you go again. Those novels and movies and all those dreary heroines with moonlight in their eyes. Hooey. Listen, Fat Ass. You realize a good piece of ass would have straightened them all out? You realize that if Heath-

72

cliffe had banged Cathy properly, she never would have mooned around the moors for him? Or that if Romeo had had at least one crack at Juliet, neither of them would have wound up dead at the ripe old age of sixteen? Bah, humbug!"

She laughed, her giggling sound.

"Listen to Scrooge talking."

"You mean *Screwwwge*, don't you?"

"Uh huh." She cradled my splendor next to her face and patted it and kissed it. A tingling sensation started all over again. Damn her ass but she was good at it. "Wish I really could speak from experience. Couldn't we at least try a back-scuttle?"

"No dice. I'd ruin you. And your health does come first."

"Kill-joy," she sniggered. But she understood and in the understanding lay our great *Rappaport* as she liked to say.

I poured us two drinks, balanced the glasses on my naked chest and she took one, downing it at a feverish gulp. Her eyes shone and she licked her shapely lips with the tongue that was one in a million.

"Roddy?"

"Mmmmmm." I was feeling much better. The drink was warming and so was her left hand which was absently but expertly toying among the non-wasteland of my crotch.

"You think this spy business is really serious?"

"What do you mean?"

"Hell, I don't know what I mean. But if all these characters do get in, all of them, what would it really accomplish? I mean there must be hundreds of enemy agents in the country all the time and nobody gets into too much of a tizzy. What's the beef now?"

"My dear girl—"

"Well, tell me. I'd really like to know."

I stared at the ceiling. My patriotism is a latent thing, I suppose. I am constantly amazed at how it pours out of me sometimes at the most unguarded moments. Maybe I talk better with all my clothes off. Most people do. They say the talk around nudist colonies is A-1.

73

"This is the greatest country in the world. We have all the four freedoms despite what happens in places like Alabama and Mississippi. The point is what does happen to the Negro there is against the law—it's *not on the books* to punish them or deny them the way Adolph did the Jews. But I digress—the point is this. Anytime there is a chance that creeps and crumbs and others can get into this country and go to work undermining what this country is, we must all see red, white and blue. Whether it's Commie or Red Chinese or an invasion of Japanese beetles. Important? Of course, it's important. We are still the hope of the world, Fat Ass. 'Twas ever thus. And come that beautiful day when all the universe is one big happy family, you'll find us somewhere in the setup. Amen and do you want another drink?"

Her eyes were shining like stars now. She bent and kissed me. I tingled in appreciation.

"Roddy, Roddy," she crooned. "You're beautiful . . . I love you . . . I love the stars and stripes forever. . . ."

"Long may it wave," I hiccuped. She giggled again.

"Long may this wave," she sighed and took me in her two warm hands and slid down to the ball line before she gave me her sweetest and most generous bite. I soared. Higher and higher. Filling her mouth with a golden me. I felt much, much better. Sex, the great healer. Kicks, the best medicine.

I was fond of Doreen. Very fond.

I just didn't know how much until the next day.

Then it was too late to tell her or show her.

Because by that fatal time, she was dead.

Butchered and violated in the worst possible way.

Thank God, that last night, we had a marvelous time. Something to warm her with on her way to the Pearly Gates. With her adorably fat ass, they certainly were going to have to widen them—

The local cops called the university about seven o'clock the next day. I was in the gymnasium showing a class of boys and girls how important physical fitness is in maintaining a happy sex life. The late hour meant nothing. It

74

was any-hour and all-hours when Damon was dealing out the instruction. When I was asked to come down to the Police Morgue to identify a fat girl who had been found murdered in an alleyway, I knew with a dread certainty that the sky is up that I would find Doreen Doremus. There had been no identification on her, the cops said, but her age and a school ring had allowed them to put two and two together. So they tried the university first.

I rode in a squad car down to the morgue. I couldn't think. My brain was numb. I knew spying was a deadly game, that nobody played fair, and when you lost the game, you usually died. You think all those things, but when something finally does happen, you go into a state of shock, paralysis that makes the whole world go blank.

I don't think I remember the building, the morgue or the cops and doctors I saw down there. All I know is that they parked me in front of a sliding drawer in an air-cooled room and then there was a grating noise. And then me staring down at the battered, beaten hulk of a naked Doreen Doremus. Her lovely face was a twisted travesty of what it had been. There was a large, unholy gash across one of her mountainous breasts, the left one, I think.

I must have flipped my cookies or almost done so. Because I do remember being helped to a chair and a quiet, authoritative voice was soberly speaking in my ear. Someone was taking notes behind me. Probably the cops who had brought me down. Or one of them, at any rate. The back of my neck was warm, my temples buzzed and the lights in the room were wavering. I felt like I was on a cheap drunk.

"Then you recognize her, Professor Damon?"

I had to answer. Talking made everything somehow different. Less difficult to believe.

"Her name's Doreen Doremus. We called her Fat Ass."

"I see. Does she have any close relatives?"

"No. She's an orphan. A big fat dead little orphan—"

"Please, Professor. We know how you feel. Shocking way to go. One of the most brutal crimes I have ever witnessed."

I looked up at that. The numbness, the faintness swept away. Blind cold rage made me like ice now. I saw the doctor's face. It was a nice friendly face. I could talk to this man.

"How brutal?" I asked.

He tried to be kind but the words just hit me like knives going in, one at a time. And each of them hurt like hell.

"She was literally assaulted and violated to death. By more than one man, most likely. Worst case I've ever seen. Apart from the damage done to her vagina, I think it brought on a heart attack. But we don't know for sure until we have a full autopsy. As for the note, well—"

"Note. What note?"

"The killer or killers were fiends. They pinned a note to her left breast. That's the gash you saw. It was very crudely done. Also, it shows the work of a maniac or maniacs."

I got to my feet. I didn't need the morgue anymore. Or the smells, or the sounds. I buttoned up my overcoat. I looked at the kindly, friendly neighborhood mortician. Why are they always so damn cheerful looking?

"May I see this note?"

"That's up to the officers—"

I turned on one of the bluecoats taking notes. He looked at his partner, shrugged, and then dug a scrap of paper out of his pocket. It was a sheaf of scrap paper, maybe five by eight, the kind you find on office desks all over the country. On it, somebody had printed in crude black block lettering, the following message:

WE DON'T WANT HER YOU CAN HAVE HER SHE'S TOO FAT FOR US. ALL THAT MEAT AND NO POTATOES.

THE GLEE CLUB

What a lousy joke. A lousy singing joke. For a moment, my eyeballs blazed, my fists knotted and I was on the point of ripping the thing to shreds when one of the cops moved fast and grabbed the thing from me.

76

"Easy, Professor. That's evidence."

"Sorry. I lost my head—"

"That's okay. Think nothing of it. Want us to drive you back to the university? We're satisfied with the identification. And don't worry. We'll find these characters, all right."

I nodded. "No, thanks. I'll get back all right. Tell me. Where did you find her?"

"Alley next to the Bowling Alley on Flood Street downtown. Dark there. Just a night light over the back door. The manager found her when he went out into the alley for a breath of fresh air. Don't know how he expected to get that in a smelly alley."

I shook my head. "This Bowling Alley—is it anywhere near a travel agency?"

The cop thought and shook his head.

"No, this is down by the seamier side of town. Just bars and clip joints. No travel agency but the one that's about ten blocks further uptown. Why?"

"Nothing. I don't know. Thanks, boys. Guess I'll go back now. She had a lot of friends at the university. They have a right to know about this—"

"Keep cool, Professor. You'll get over this."

"Maybe——"

When I got out of that morgue and that building, I began to walk aimlessly. I was headed toward the university, of course, but that austere edifice was at least five miles away in the outer part of town. It had begun to rain and it pelted down on me while my head was humming with hangover, agony and doubt and fear. It is hard to assimilate the death of anyone, let alone a dear friend, on such short notice. When it's a jolly fat girl whom you have balled for good fun and kicks and pleasure, it's like a shocking dash of cold water.

Water.

I staggered down the darkening streets. The rain kept on coming down. I was hatless but I never noticed it. All I noticed was that I was choked with a sense of loss and that tears were streaming down my face. If Walrus-moustache could only see me now.

77

I was cryin' in the rain.

And the murderous, fiendish men who had signed their names as *The Glee Club* wouldn't do anymore singing if I ever caught up with them. I would slice their balls off and feed them to the biggest rodents I could find in the university basement.

Damn all spies everywhere.

And murderers who balled poor helpless fat girls to death. That was not a lovely way to go. Not for Doreen Doremus. Not for anybody. I was crying, but honest to God I felt like I could eat nails.

I was mad enough to do some killing of my own.

But you can't kill somebody you can't see or find. Somebody you don't know. Nobody can do that.

Not even a Rod Damon can do that.

All I could do, for the time being, was cry.

I did enough of that on the way back to my rooms at the university. And I hadn't cried since the day when I found out that the Dragon Lady in the *Terry And The Pirates* comic strip wasn't a real live girl whose address was in the telephone book.

CHAPTER EIGHT

Doreen Doremus' death, as they say, was only the beginning. There were more things in heaven and hell and in the United States than I ever dreamed of in my Sex Philosophy, Horatio. But forget Hamlet. The Big Spy Hunt Affair turned into an omelet of disastrous proportions. I'm afraid I went a little berserk, adding confusion and pell-mell activity to my list of sins. I just felt I had to be doing something. I wasn't fooled by *The Glee Club* killers. The cops and the law agencies were thinking in terms of just a nasty homicide. But I knew, I *knew* that Doreen Doremus had been killed because she was hot on the spy trail. But I had to keep that to myself. Walrus-moustache and his Security measures. But I guess he was right. Why muck things up?

I rounded up my six subordinate Junior James Bonds

and gave it to them straight from the shoulder. No more tears for Doreen Doremus; one of them had been cut down by the enemy and it was up to them to make that enemy pay. A real pep talk I gave them, but all the time I was wishing we were all somewhere else. Like say in Hawaii, surfing and sexing and cutting up generally. Cutting up the right way.

Yet, I wasn't prepared for their heat, their ardor, their devotion to duty. Or their fever for revenge.

"We'll get those bastards," Adele Ash towered her six feet into the air and there was a grim look on her cute kisser. She made ripping and tearing motions with her fingers. Her eyes were screwy.

Corinne Murphy poked her forty-two chest at me. Her eyes were still washed out from all the crying she had done at Doreen's funeral. "Poor Fat Ass. She died a virgin. The worst kind of thing that can happen to a woman." Amen to that.

I made no comment and looked at Pete Porter and Tony Eden. Both the football heroes were coldly silent, their big shoulders and shaggy heads lowered. Like bulls ready to charge. Tony Eden was tossing a coin *a la* George Raft, without looking up. As if he felt guilty about his AC-DC circuit around town. He had been plenty busy.

Norma Davis and Alice Potter, still doing the twin routine, were hugging each other, sobbing softly into each other's hair. It was a sad scene all around, this session. So I told them to be careful, watch their asses, and sent them on their way. They marched out like an army.

About ten minutes later, there was a knock at my door. I said "Come on in" even though I was distracted by examining some charts which showed the varied and divergent sexual level of responses in men and women who have just passed the age of consent. If there was a Generation Gap, I was out to find it. As well as find spies.

Rita Cortez sashayed into the room. She stalked in like a cougar on the prowl. She was wearing a blue Bolero jacket, mini-skirt with stripes and low loafers which made her walk as silent as that same cougar. The Hong Kong Flu hadn't hurt her a bit. She was as white-skinned, black-haired, red-lipped and humpable as ever. Her figure was really unique. She could have been measured out with a set of calipers and come out even on both sides to the thousandth of an inch. Her green eyes undressed me, almost mockingly.

"You wanted to see me?"

"I wanted to see you three weeks ago. After Lights Out. But that will have to wait. Yeah, I wanted to see you."

She placed a pink tongue on her lower lip. Her wham-whams, high, tilted and perfectly round, pushed out at me.

"Whatever I can do for you, Professor Damon—will be an honor."

"Sure. How would you like to be my *Aide de Sex?*"

Her black eyebrows V'd in surprise. But she smiled.

"I am yours to command. But first tell me what you mean?"

I put the charts aside and walked around her. She stood perfectly still and straight as I surveyed her goodies. I placed my hands on her flanks, squeezed gently and repeated the performance on her arched bosom. She was real, all right. Anything more real would have been fantasy. I curbed the rising heat in my loins and got down to business. Walrus-moustache's kind of business.

"It's a cover title, actually. Oh, you can assist me in sexual matters, but right now I'm short one member of my team. You will have heard about it somehow, I suppose, but I'll take a chance. What do you think of the idea of being a lady spy for me?"

Her green eyes squinted. But not because she needed glasses.

"Oh," she said. "Doreen Doremus. The poor fat girl——"

"Yes. But let me explain the whole scene to you. Then you can make up your own mind. I don't want them pinning notes to your—ah—body, too." I gave her the whole pitch, from Walrus-moustache on up to the inglorious present. The stuff about windburns and Mexico got her, as I knew it would. Why shouldn't it? Latins are Latins no matter what part of the globe they call home.

"As I said, Professor Damon, it is a privilege to be asked. I say Yes. Without reservations. Where would you like me to begin?"

"On the bed in there, to tell the truth and shame the prudes, but it will have to wait." I took my eyes off the faint pulse throbbing in that delicious neck of hers. I had a wild idea what a session with this ex-call girl might be like. A real Puerto Rican hayride, I fancied. But there were things to be done. Spy things. Sex things would have to come later.

Rita Cortez glanced toward the bedroom. When she looked back at me, it was with a tremor running through her body. All her splendid assets pulsed with life and animation.

"I too look forward, Professor, to a meeting with you as man and woman. The seventh method was a delight but it hardly compensated for my missing our tryst that night. The Hong Kong Flu—I didn't want you to catch my germs—"

"Don't remind me. And you can call me Rod when we are alone like this."

"Very well. Rod. An apt title considering your abilities——"

"Sure, sure. Now are you ready to start work? I have a hot lead. Something Doreen was working on when they—well, will you or won't you?"

She laughed, the white teeth flashing.

"Must I say Yes more than once? I told you. I am ready, *now*."

She certainly was. The Bolero jacket was vibrating, her sensuous hips snaked out toward me and her red mouth pouted. While it's true I could easily emulate Speedy Gonzales and knock off a piece in no time at all, I wanted the grand full treatment with Rita Cortez. Like, say, later that night when the university was closed down and maybe even the spies were sleeping or making love. I didn't want any interruptions when I began my campaign on her. I had about a thousand things to try. Besides, I was still feeling my sorrow about Doreen Doremus. And not even

81

I have ever gotten laid so soon after a funeral. I do have my respects for the dead.

"Good girl. Now here's my plan—"

She listened, nodding, writing down names of places and addresses and I marveled at her easy acceptance of a dangerous assignment. The girl had guts, obviously. I was sending her right into the lion's den. No mistake about that. When I had finished with all the details, I ran a vocal test just to make sure she understood what I was asking her to do. She looked like a quick learner. A fact worth remembering. Out of bed or in it.

"All right, Rita. Now spell out for me what you're going to do. There must be no slip-ups. These characters play for keeps."

"My father was a *torero* in Madrid," she said proudly, "and my mother a lady wrestler. I have learned all the methods of self-defense. Don't worry about me. As a call girl in Puerto Rico, I had to handle many a brutal male customer. You would be surprised the things some of them asked me to do—*disgusting.*"

Now I felt like Walrus-moustache usually felt talking to me.

"Spare me the sordid details. Just tell me what you're going to do as per my instructions."

She nodded, and consulted her notes.

"I am to attire myself in my most provocative clothing, go to the travel agency at the address given here and make myself known to the people there as a woman interested in all arrivals and departures to and from Mexico. I am looking for a cousin, Pedro Garcia, whom I expect any day. He is Cuban. Then I am to meet you in the Bowling Alley on Flood Street at ten o'clock. To tell you what I have learned or to indicate if anyone has followed me from the travel agency."

"On the nose. Just remember don't stick your neck out or try to make like *The Girl From U.N.C.L.E.* I don't want any more dead heroines. Clear? All we have to do is flush some of these spies out into the open. I have other people and agencies who can do the rough work."

"As you say. I will mind my manners. As for the provocative clothes, I have just the thing. A blue-sheath mini-dress that is no more than a Bikini, actually. Do you think that will do?"

"Wear anything. Wear what you got on now. You'd look provocative in a paper bag, I must say. Well, we're all set. I want you to start on this right away. I've got a pass for you from school. If the afternoon gets boring around that travel agency, read a book or something."

"I shall." Her eyes were mocking again. "I have a well-thumbed copy of *Furnishings and Furniture: Their Erotic Importance in Love-Making.* Perhaps you know the author? Professor Rod Damon?"

I smiled. Now I knew how she had gotten 100 on her thesis.

"One of my best works. If you remember the section on chairs and ottomans, I should like to demonstrate for you some time."

Her eyes stared straight into mine. *"Anytime,* Rod."

"Tonight then. After you finish your first expedition in the field. Okay?"

"Yes. I should like that. Very much. I must confess I am burning with curiosity about you. The time has come to know you better. Much better." She moistened her lips for me. They gleamed like blood.

I lost my head. I grabbed her. It was that damn red mouth, those green eyes, those knockers, those hips, that Snow White skin. I gathered all of her charms into me and rammed her mouth with mine. She was ready for me. She parted her lips and her pink tongue snaked and I lost the play. She made me smoke up like Dante's Inferno in ten seconds flat. When I was through brushing her lithe body with my own, she stepped back, pulling away. She was out of breath. Her ivory skin was tinged with a delectable shade of crimson. The pulse in her throat jumped and her writhing mammaries settled down.

I straightened my tie and tried to ignore the rude erection which had sprung into being. She couldn't miss it and she didn't.

"Madre!" she whispered. "You are indeed a giant among men. Never have I seen or known such a thing—"

83

"It's no thing," I said evenly, composing myself. "Even if it's my own thing. It's just little old me."

"Don't be ridiculous," she said, with a trace of anger. "It's a monument, a peninsula, a promontory—"

"You've been reading *Cyrano de Bergerac*," I rasped. "Go on. Get out of here before I flip you and deck you before you get out of this room. Vamoose, Rita. See you later."

She showed me her teeth again.

"*You* will *see*, later," she promised.

On the challenge, she turned around and sashayed out of the room. Walking, standing or sitting down or kneeling, she was a tone poem of sexuality, carnality and just plain *Tiger!* The cougar in her was all in the movement and it was the cat family all the way to the door. When she was finally gone, I had to think of something else to make my heat go down. I was on fire, inflamed with thoughts of her and me and the big, wide bed inside that overlooked the campus grounds. I'd be tentpoling tonight with her or I would commit suicide. I had to have this broad before another day dawned. Seldom have I been teased so long and so hard by merely one female. It wasn't usual at all. Clovis Lee had filled my need, poor Fat Ass had helped and along the route toward all the trouble, Rita Cortez had had the Hong Kong Flu. But now the Flu was gone and the only flaw in my plans was my guilty need to use her first as a spy. The loving had to be delayed.

Tony Eden stuck his head in my door while I was back on the charts, still measuring sexual response figures and manfully putting Rita Cortez and her body to one side.

"Hi, Prof. Got a sec?"

"Sure, Tony. Come in."

He practically pranced into the room, his eyes lit up with that thing they call dedication. Or purposefulness. Or just plain old determination. He was a Four-Letter man, but now the letters were K-I-L-L.

"You look bright-eyed and bushy-tailed," I said. "What gives?"

"I got a hot lead, Prof. I want to follow it up right

84

away. You want to listen?" His voice was anxious, eager-to-get-going.

"That's what I'm here for. Shoot."

"Okay. I'm squiring Corinne Murphy to a club in town. *The Alarm Clock*. It's a tweety-bird dive and from what I've found out, there's been a lot of Mexicans and guys with sunburns hanging around. Sounds good, if you ask me. Okay with you?"

"You bet. But watch yourself. And Corinne. I know you're both big enough to clean out a barroom but these birds are playing for keeps. Remember Doreen."

"I do," he said, with a bold look in his blue eyes. "That's why I'll do anything to get the bastards that killed her. Just wanted you to know."

"Thanks. Good luck. And holler for me if you need help."

"Check. See you, Prof." He ran out of the room like he was beginning a running broad jump. Youth. Youth. Eager to live. Eager to serve. Eager to get in on the act. Any act. When I went back to my work, I was feeling pretty damn teary about the whole thing. Doreen's death had hit me even harder than I thought. I really liked that fat-assed broad. A lot.

But again, the mess was only just beginning. There were far worse things in the offing. The carnival of killing had just begun.What I didn't know or realize was that Walrus-moustache had walked me into the messiest, most gruesome caper of my entire career as Coxeman. I've seen my share of naked bodies, the living and the dead, but I had no idea or notion of the blood bath which had fallen over the university. How could I? It was beyond comprehension for a man whose greatest interest in life lies in the pursuit and tattooing of lovely available women. I'm an optimist all the way. I don't see the hole in the doughnut.

I worked on the charts until it was time to close up shop. The daylight left the windows and I prepared myself for the rendezvous with Rita Cortez. I shaved, showered, made myself a light dinner and read over my notes. I was feeling a little better about everything. But not much better. A pall still hung over me. I was a little restless and moody. Even when Clovis Lee materialized after seven o'clock in her Baby Doll, her willingness and a new clever thing she had thought of in regard to one of our positions, I was barely in the mood to love her. But I did anyway. I'm afraid I hurt her a little. I dropped down on her from the forty-five degree position and practically hammered her back into the sheets and pillows. She came yearningly back at me for more, bruised and beaten, but still willing to try some other things. I was listless and hardly paid any attention as she sat on me and worked herself up and down. When she had dampened my whole abdomen with her enthusiasm, I called Time and said I had to be going. I had an important appointment.

I guess she understood. Almost meekly, she climbed into her Baby Doll and sauntered out of the room. She didn't look back and her shoulders were twitching as if she was crying quietly to herself.

Even sexpots find a way to go into mourning. It was a tribute to Doreen Doremus that even a flaming wild one like Clovis Lee could acknowledge her passing by closing up shop on her desires. I thought about that as I got ready to go meet Rita Cortez at the Bowling Alley on Flood Street.

I checked the address from the big, thick telephone directory on my night stand. Flood Street wasn't exactly one of the choicest neighborhoods in the city. It was no garden spot. Look at what had happened to Doreen Doremus in its tainted atmosphere. Still, it was the only real clue to the situation. The travel agency might turn out to be a dead end, and maybe Tony Eden and Corinne Murphy would be wasting their time and their charms at *The Alarm Clock*, but the spy game is a lot like the Sex game. You have to try everything. See what happens. Experience is the best teacher.

And sometimes you get the worst marks because of that.

Seven little students standing in line, all wanting to get into the act, and doing just fine—spying in the sticks.

One got herself banged to death and then there were six—

86

Six little students acting like a beehive.

Buzzing all around the place and then there were five—

I pushed the horrible little poem from my mind, raced down the university steps under cover of darkness and went to the parking area where my little Renault waited for me.

A gift from my Paris adventure from the *Academie Sexualité* but that had really been a tourist's ball compared to what was coming up on the bill of fare.

Like I said. Little did I know.

Me and *Rebecca* of Manderly.

CHAPTER NINE

The Bowling Alley on Flood Street was a surprise and a half. It was closed! There was a sign on the door that said: CLOSED DUE TO DEATH IN THE FAMILY. And there wasn't a light or a soul around for miles. Somebody had a lousy sense of humor. The police might have padlocked the place because of Doreen Doremus' murder but I doubted that very much. It was a cinch she had had no relations working in the Bowling Alley, either. The watch on my wrist said ten o'clock on the nose and I wondered if Rita Cortez had come and gone. It wasn't likely. She would have waited at least a few minutes.

It was a warm night with no stars in the sky and the part of town I was in was so corrupt and out of the way, there weren't many people abroad on the streets. The only broads there would have been would certainly have been hookers. Far up the block the lights of a few bars glowed dimly and there was a slight undercurrent of vaguely heard jukebox music and raucous laughter. Typical bar noises. I waited in the darkened doorways of the Bowling Alley and made myself blend with the shadows. It was a spooky feeling, doing this James Bond routine. No, that isn't right either. That cat lived it up with great girls, fancy gambling casinos, rich villas in the hills. This was Dragsville, U.S.A. A real Doctor No-No or Gold-platedfinger!

It got to be about ten twenty and I was beginning to worry about Rita Cortez when I heard the scream. A woman's scream. Just a long, low shriek of womanly noise that sounded like a cat being stepped on. Or a pussy— it set the short hairs of my neck on the full rise going up.

I didn't stop to think. The sound came from inside the Bowling Alley. I put my shoulder to the doors, kicked and lo and behold!—they fell open just like they do in the movies. I rushed in.

The scream came again, off and to my right. In the darkness and with hardly a gleam of light, I ran toward the sound. I bumped into something, cursed, and kept on going. Suddenly I could hear a flurry of voices—men's voices—and the woman crying out again. No mistake this close—it was Rita Cortez!

Ever stumble around a pitch-black bowling alley you've never been in before? It's fun, I can tell you. All I had to guide me were the sound of guys having a good wild time and some dame—it had to be Rita—yelling and moaning like a banshee. I don't know how I did it, but I finally badly navigated across that floor until I found a flight of steps. By that time, the alarm had been given because I'd made such a helluva racket and the jig was up. And the fun was over. A door opened somewhere above and light spilled out, blinding me. And then so help me a goddam troop of guys came flying out of that room, down the stairs, running into me, trying to bowl on by and bowl me over. I didn't know what I was doing. I started to swing wildly, pushing my right and left fist into a lot of bodies and faces. I scored a few times and then I think I really blew my cool, remembering those female screams which had now stopped and sounded like a blubbering, wailing kind of whimpering. I felt a wild rage, my strength was as of the strength of ten. I was a giant among men and I flailed out my fists like twin destroyers. I did okay too. I heard some shouts of pain as my fists landed. I could make out dark outlines going down. I kicked out, yelling, shouting and all I got back were curses and more rushing bodies. My God, there must have been an army of them. And they didn't want to have anything

88

to do with me. They wanted no part of me because I had raised a ruckus in a place supposedly closed and that must have meant nothing but trouble and cops to them. They all wanted Out in a hurry. The sooner the better.

The ranks thinned, the stairway thundered with rushing feet and I could make them all out, racing through the open double doors of the alley's front entrance. It must have taken only a few minutes, the whole fight. But suddenly I was alone on the stairs and only the echoes of the male voices and running feet lingered in the darkened game spot. My head was bruised, my fists were aching from the punches I had landed. I got myself steadied and lurched up the rest of the staircase toward that lighted door. From behind it, the feminine crying had fallen to a low moaning. Something inside me shrunk down to a peanut of hopeless despair. I didn't want to find Rita Cortez in the same shape I had found Doreen Doremus.

It was worse, actually.

Far worse.

Doreen Doremus didn't have to live with what had been done to her. Dying does have some small advantages.

Rita Cortez was alive and not well and hardly living in a university town. This was Living?

They had had her stretched across the table, backside up. Her backside. Both her excellent legs were strapped with cord to the legs of the table. By the time I got her untied and over to a dingy crumpled up bed in one corner of the room, I could see what else was wrong with her. Before she told me all about it. Right then she couldn't do anything but faint. No wonder.

As beautifully formed as her body was, as indescribably perfect all her natural architecture, it had been slobbered and drooled over by the basest brutes. She had teethmarks and bites and minor gouges all over her. Her white lovely skin was a dartboard. She reeked of semen and that odor that is only ugly and animal-like when it carries with it sights and scenes like the way she looked. She was a bad accident. I didn't have to be a sexologist to know what was wrong with her. The dopiest man on the street would

89

have known that she had obviously been through the gang-bang of this or any other year.

The room had only the bed and table and a single electric light bulb dangling over the sordid scene. No pictures, no chairs. Just the two items of furniture and assorted empty pop bottles and beer bottles. I shuddered to think they might have been used on her above and beyond their original purpose in manufacture.

I had a terrible suspicion that the *Glee Club* had sung again. They had played the same lousy terrible song: sex, sadism and brutality.

When I finally got Rita Cortez revived and found her clothes in a pile under the bed—she had worn the costume she suggested to me at the university and she was right it was no bigger than a Bikini—the whole horrible humping saga came tumbling out of her. For once, her placidly ivory face was a shocked mask of disbelief. Oh, was she glad to see me! She hugged me, raining kisses on my cheeks, nose and chin in her blind gratitude. Then I got her simmered down to the point where she could answer some questions. But I thought it a good idea to get her back into the Renault and out of all this mess before the cops came or something else happened to her. Or both of us.

What a neighborhood.

We got out of the bowling alley and into the Renault without so much as hearing a siren or seeing a passerby. The bars up the street were still playing the same old tunes and the same old laughter was ribaldly echoing. A great neighborhood to kill a man or gang-bang a girl. I'd have to mention it to my local Mafia man. What a bunch of crumbs!

After we were about a mile out of town and she had really calmed down enough to talk coherently, she gave me the whole picture. She'd hung around the travel agency, made her pitch, and come up blank. It was only when she was on her way to the part of town where the Bowling Alley was that she was suddenly kidnapped; two men, both very young, like teenagers, had wrestled her into a parked car and that was all she remembered until she

90

woke up tied to that table, with all of them taking turns. As much as she could remember, there seemed to be about ten of them. Not to mention perhaps three girls.

"Girls?" I almost put my foot through the accelerator. "Don't tell me——"

"They did," she said calmly, staring straight ahead. Her face was frozen solid. As if she could never cry again. "I have never known that women could be that way. So perverted. They kissed me, made love to me while the men watched. And then the men took their turns. I wonder if I'll ever be good for a man again . . ."

"Can that kind of talk," I growled. "You can take a helluva lot more punishment than you think."

"Can I? I wonder." Her voice was a sad instrument. Almost dead. But for all of her ghastly exercises in perversion, she still looked better than all the women in the world.

"Don't be foolish. You know the average happily married housewife makes love all her life? Sometimes, night after night. Nothing can wear out a vagina unless it's constantly abused, misused and generally badly handled. This one bad night won't kill you. You'll see."

For a moment, her breasts rose with a sigh.

"You're the professor," she said. "I'll try to believe you."

I changed the subject. "Sorry about this. I knew it was dangerous. But I didn't think they'd make a move so soon after Doreen. Which means we're on the right track. Tell me, Rita. Didn't you see or hear anything at all that might be a lead in tracking down these gangbangers?"

She shuddered. "I am sorry—I was in such a state of shock and terror, everything was a blur. I guess I'm pretty much of a disappointment to you as an, what did you call it—?"

"*Aide de sex* and you're just fine. I'm proud of you."

"Thank you. That is something, at least."

"Big deal," I growled. "In one night, I nearly got you killed on the job."

"That was my fault. I should have been more careful."

"Maybe. I'm not so sure. I think we're batting our heads

91

against a stone wall. This is a whole lot bigger than I thought. Than even Washington, D.C., thought. I'm only good for running classes on Sex and men and women, but when it comes to making like a master espionage agent, I'm a bust."

She put her hand on my knee, still with her eyes in steady concentration on the road. My headlights were stabbing the dark ribbon of highway leading back to the university.

"Do not demean yourself, Rod. You're probably doing better than even you think. Than anybody could. You'll see."

"I wonder," I said, trying to forget what had happened to Doreen Doremus and to her.

Under the circumstances, one thing after the other, once more my belated tryst with Rita Cortez was postponed. I was running out of rainchecks. But honestly, how could I think of Sex after a night like she had had? I'm only human but I'm no heel, either. Or as much of a sex fiend as Walrus-moustache makes me out to be.

So I took her home to the university nestling among the pines and aspens, kissed her goodnight and went back up to my own rooms. The joint was fast asleep and no one was patrolling the halls. Rita Cortez looked grateful when I let her wander back to her own part of the building. She looked *so* grateful to me I felt as noble as King Arthur and Charlie Brown of the Peanuts comic strip. I had done my good deeds for the day. I had saved her from a death worse than fate and I had abstained like Hamlet wanted his old lady Gertrude to do. There are such men, sometimes.

But it was one of those days when nothing goes right.

I'd no sooner barred my front door to keep Clovis Lee from dropping in and settled down in bed with a copy of *Portnoy's Complaint* to keep my mind off things when the phone rang. Just by the sound of the damn thing, I knew it was a headache coming up.

It wasn't Clovis or Rita or Walrus-moustache or any of my kids, the spies. It was the Police Department and I had a funny feeling I was talking to the same cop who

92

had given me the dope on Doreen Doremus. It was. He introduced himself as Johnson and got right to the point.

"Sorry about this, Professor. We want you to come down to the morgue to identify a body. Kid named Tony Eden. Do you know the name? We found his university ID in his wallet——"

"Oh, no——" The blood raced around in my head. My ears hummed.

"I know how you feel. Looks like open season on college kids. Another rough one. We found Eden down by the docks, lying across a pile of timbers. Naked as a jaybird. I'm afraid they sliced him pretty bad."

"Don't spare the details. Let's have it."

Johnson seemed to cough. It sounded like a cough.

"They or whoever it was, cut off his whatsit and took it with them. It was nowhere around the vicinity of the body. Eden bled to death."

"The sonsofbitches," I muttered. "Give me a half-hour. I'll be there as soon as I can——" Then I remembered he was going down to that club, *The Alarm Clock* with stacked Corinne Murphy. My blood ran cold. "Tell me, Johnson. A girl named Corinne Murphy. Tall, built like Liz Taylor. A brunette. She isn't——?"

Johnson was definite on that one.

"No dolls around him. He was alone. Maybe you got something you can tell us about all this, Professor?"

"Talk to you when I get there. See you."

I hung up. I stared at the phone. I cursed fluently. I ground my fists into my face. I kicked the floor. I didn't cry. The rage in me was something for the books. I wanted to scream out at the world and call everybody a dirty name. Up to and including Walrus-moustache, flag and country.

But I got dressed again in an icy seething fury that enabled me to get out of my room and down to Police Headquarters in twenty minutes by the clocks. They had cut Tony Eden's pecker off and left him to die by inches and somebody was going to pay for it. Pay all the way.

And I had to stop whoever it was before they decimated my entire corps of amateur spies. Amateurs was right.

93

Me included.

The biggest amateur of all.

What a laugh.

Rod Damon, Master Spy.

Rod Damon, Butcher, was more like it.

Maybe Portnoy had a lot to complain about with his Jewish hangups and his sexual problems but he had nothing on me. I was running way ahead of him. I had a right to sing the blues.

Everybody I knew and liked was getting knocked off! What a way to run a spyline!

CHAPTER TEN

WE WANTED A BASS AND WE WOUND UP WITH A LOUSY TENOR. WE'RE GONNA BEEF TO THE UNION.

THE GLEE CLUB

That was the lousy note the cops found clutched in Tony Eden's left hand. The Glee Club was complaining too. Damn their souls. A look at Tony in the Morgue was even less pleasant, if that's the word, than my last look at Doreen Doremus. A pecker-less corpse is not recommended for stomachs and imaginations like mine. Johnson had to help me into the next room again and once more, the cheerful-faced doctor gave me a slug of rye. It burned my throat but it made me feel better.

Johnson and his fellow officers were in a quandary. What was going on? College pranks? Sadistic initiations? A gang war between rival fraternities? And who was this Corinne Murphy kid I said was missing? You can imagine the spot I was in. There I was, Secret Agent Damon, sworn to secrecy by the twisted rules of the game and I had to dummy up for the Law and pretend to be the innocent bystander. I could see Johnson and his pals were a mite skeptical. But what could they do to me?

Nothing.

94

What the Glee Club did to Corinne Murphy was something else again.

Her body was found one day later—not in a bowling alley nor on a pile of timbers on a pier—but in a different part of town. High up in the suburbs in a swanky lobby of a high-class apartment house. There was no note this time. There didn't have to be. Corinne Murphy had been sliced up from top to bottom with something that must have been a Bowie knife. The slices were that large. And the wildest figure since Liz Taylor was something for the dogs in the alley. But the Glee Club had outdone themselves.

Tony Eden's whatsit, as Johnson had euphemistically named it, was neatly stuffed into her dead red mouth.

I was getting to be a steady customer at the Morgue. A shot of rye didn't help this time. I tossed my cookies all over the place. Also, I panicked. I can take a hint. My rat pack of spies was marked for the black spot. Doreen, Tony, Corinne and a near-miss on Rita—did I need a building to fall on me? Death marked the spot and me and Adele Ash, Alice Potter, Norma Davis and Pete Porter were standing right on it!

Johnson felt he had been patient with me long enough. He was seriously contemplating a third degree and the rack for me when he was mysteriously summoned to the phone. He was gone about fifteen minutes when he came back, looking mad as a wet dog, and grunted to his subordinates: "Take the Professor back to college. He's free to go. We'll keep in touch, won't we, Professor?"

I wasn't fooled by his charity.

Walrus-moustache had obviously pulled some strings. He kept me out of jail as a material witness and he also kept the murdering spree out of the newspapers. The way it worked out, only the people at the university and a handful of cops knew what was going on. And of course, the Glee Club—and their Chinese Red bosses.

I'm afraid I panicked in the wrong direction. I am not clever, I am not brainy. I need a refuge, a way out, a different room to think in. Desperately, hungrily, I called on Adele Ash when I got back from the Morgue. To tell

95

the truth, I wanted to hide out from Walrus-moustache. I was really afraid I'd throttle him if I ever saw him again. He was the one that had gotten me into this. The only one.

She was doing her Yoga exercises when I got there. Being a six-footer, she was well aware of the weight she was carrying around and she kept fit. Wow, did she keep fit. Never was six foot of dame so well distributed and spaced for loving mankind. When I saw her, in her brief wisp of Bikini and two bra patches, like a burlesque queen's pasties, my heart went out to her. She'd be perfect for what ailed me.

Rita Cortez was still recovering from her ordeal, something a trifle worse than the Flu Hong Kong, Clovis Lee I had wearied of and besides she was always crying now and of course, Doreen was no more—

"Professor!" Adele Ash said brightly, "grab a couple of Indian clubs and toughen your muscles up. You look a little pale—"

I had balled Adele in the long ago, but so many girls and faces and bodies had followed her in happy succession that I couldn't remember if she was a good lay or not. She certainly *looked* like a good lay.

She was the honey-blonde from Milwaukee and her body was a golden synchronization of breasts, hips, thighs and legs. She also had a directness of speech and manner that was refreshing. I knew it was too early for her to know about Tony Eden and Corinne Murphy and I saw no reason to bring corpses into the subject.

"I don't want Indian clubs," I said. "I want you."

She slid down from her Yoga position, came up on her haunches as pretty as a picture and snapped erect. She was flushed, barely out of breath and her yum-yums were rising and falling nicely. She shook her head. "I don't get it, Professor."

"Get what?"

She shrugged and reached for a towel to dry herself. There was a nice big bed in the room. By the window with the shadows of pines and aspens filling the eye.

"You could have had me a dozen times but you were always busy with other people. 'Course I can't kick. I

96

was balling Tony and Pete but—you horsed around with that Clovis Lee and then poor Doreen you threw a bone now and then and anybody with half an eye could see your tongue was hanging out for that Puerto Rican tomcat. Now you walk in here and pick me out? What's the angle?"

"Angle? Do I need one?"

Her eyes glittered and fell down to my waistline. "No, not really, to tell the truth. Shall I get ready or are you going to warm me up a little first?"

This was my kind of woman, my kind of talk. I felt fifty percent better.

"How do you want it?" I smiled. "Medium, rare or well-done?"

"Well-done, if you please. Pete and Tony been scarce since yesterday morning and I am hurting a little."

I felt a stab of worry. I knew well enough what had happened to Tony Eden but where the hell was Pete Porter? But I stopped thinking about him before I got to the verge of a nervous breakdown.

"Kill the lights, lock the door, and join me on the bed," I commanded. "In the altogether, if you please." I stripped myself as I walked to the bed. When I let myself down on the soft percales, I stretched myself out and waited for her. I was down to the buff and it felt marvelous. In a quick moment, the room was in semi-darkness. I saw her tall, filled-out silhouette poised above me, standing alongside the bed. Cooling hands reached down and touched me. Her slender strong fingers began a mild massage. I reached up with my hands, took both her extraordinary mammaries in my hands and squeezed.

"Oh," she said, sounding almost like a little girl. "Don't do that—not so soon—"

"Why?"

"Anybody plays with those," she whispered, leaning over until they were brushing against my warm face, "gets to home plate in a hurry . . ."

"Suppose I'm anxious to score?"

"Then it's your time at bat, Professor."

Boy, she was clever. Wow, do I teach them good! The

97

kind of wanton, willful patter she was dishing out is what makes all grown men grow bigger. Presto, my head began to swell. She could feel it too. It was poking into her ribs, just under the superb overhang of breast. I parted her thighs with my right hand and she was straddling me. I didn't feel like getting off my back. I didn't feel like clever sexual games or bold variations or experiments. I just wanted to get laid. Properly or improperly; whichever way Adele Ash wanted it. She had a right to be happy too. Tomorrow, she could be dead if I didn't change my lousy tactics. Or Walrus-moustache didn't send for the U.S. Marines.

I worked my hands into her deep valley of femininity. She shuddered and widened the bridge of her thighs even further. The hanging gardens were rammed to my lips now and I was gently, then hungrily kissing them. Biting them. I heard her moan; I heard her cry out in jungle ecstasy and then impatiently, hurriedly, past all coolness, she was straddling me with her knees flanking me and both her hands guiding me into the balanced beauty of her own Valley of the Shadows.

I thrust.

She exploded.

Being very big is one thing. Not killing the girl or simply filling her so that she feels overstuffed and incapable of moving or enjoying herself is something else. I'd been down that road too many times to bungle it. She appreciated the difference and she knew how to handle it. She was a fine student.

With her first hungry orgasm out of the way, she settled into a rhythmic rocking motion that held me, receded a bit, held me again and then gradually worked up to the fever pitch that indicates another big coming. She never got too far away from me. I had both her boobs anchored in each hand and I could touch out my strength and always haul her back in. I'm big enough for that too.

Something she realized and appreciated with great quivering gusts of air and rapid murmuring sighs and yesses. There wasn't a No in her. She was the kind that only says "NO!" when she feels you about to leave her.

98

We pumped rhythmically. I felt like ten men again. Why not? I was in the racket I knew best; the place I loved the most: my own *bête noire*, the divided path of a woman's thighs, which is to me the road to the Emerald City, Shangri-la and Utopia all rolled into one.

"Rod, Rod, Rod. . . ." Her voice was on the rise, timed to that next big one that should have been heard all over the building.

"Adele, Adele, Adele. . . ." I kept the rhythm with her.

"Oh, my Milwaukee ass!" She suddenly let out a low scream. "Now, please now—NOW!"

It was easy to oblige. She was warm, bursting, heavenly. I opened the doors of the dam and we both washed away on a flood of bright lights, waves of delight and sated passions.

We were a little quiet for a long time.

We lay side by side. She kept her hand on my tool, I remained with my fingers clamped about her breasts.

I've said it before. I'll say it again.

A raise? A promotion? A medal? A new house? Hooey. I can't think of one single momentary experience that can match a good bang with a very good girl. Sue me if you think I'm wrong. Bet the Judge throws you and your case out of court.

She doodled with her fingers. It felt nice and squirmy.

"Professor?"

"Pumpkin?"

"You really are good, you know it? You make me so —geezis, warm and crazy and nice! Pete and Tony, as big as they are, can't hold a candle to you. No wonder you're able to teach classes in Sex. You *know* what you're talking about."

"Thank you," I said humbly. "I had good instruction as a boy."

She wanted to know more about that, but I didn't want to talk about me. "Besides," I said, "you don't have to bedeck me with all the posies. A man is really only as good as the woman is. And you are some woman."

"I'm flattered."

"Be flattered. In a few more minutes, you'll be flattened.

99

I'm going topside this time. You're going to find out what dive-bombing really is."

She trembled in my arms, as big as she was. "Don't tease me."

"What do you mean?"

"You can't *really* get it up again. Not after what we just had. Nobody could. Not so soon, I mean—"

"Silly girl. This is Damon. I invented the big comeback. Don't give it another thought."

"Oh, you—why did you make me wait all this time for you to come around? That first time, I was just a rookie and you were so wild and quick and strong—you remember, my induction day here? Last year?"

"Uh huh. I remember now." I did. She had a curious little scissor kick for such a big girl. I had made notes on it.

"Listen, Adele. I heard a rumor. About Tony Eden."

"What did you hear?"

"That he's kind of gay. Likes to swing both ways. That true?"

She started to laugh. A low, girlish giggle. I waited for her to calm down.

"Then you know something?" I said.

"Nothing you could work on," she sighed. "Yeah, Young Tony has his quirks. Oh, we balled fine. Nothing wrong there. But you know what he always liked me to do?"

"That's why I'm asking. What?"

"He always wanted me to keep pinching his ass while he was on top of me. Poor baby. He's got the most black-and-blue behind in the university. I wondered about him because of that. Now that you tell me about the rumors, I'm not surprised. It struck me as a little queer—what with the little experience I've had, Lord knows."

I'd never noticed Tony Eden's rump. Not that it mattered now. But he *could* have been killed by a bunch of perverts who weren't spies and maybe the same thing happened to Rita Cortez and Doreen and poor Corinne Murphy—no, no! It had to be the Chinese Reds. What the hell was I looking for an excuse for?

100

"And Pete Porter?"

She snorted in the darkness.

"His only trouble is that he's a real animal. Wham-bam, thank you, ma'am, and then he's gotta run out to football practice or something. Are all young guys like that, Rod? They want it, they like it, but as soon as it's over, they run right out like they were leaving the scene of an accident. That's what makes a girl feel *cheap*. Nothing else."

"Youth. It's Youth. Wise of you to notice, Adele. A young man feels if he hangs around he'll get involved with the girl. Like love or marriage. So he runs. Of course, I'm talking about the way my generation acted. Your generation works it the other way around. They pretend extreme indifference and sloppiness and work it out that way. Good for Pete Porter. An old-fashioned boy, obviously. He'll learn how to sit around and enjoy it, sooner or later. At least, he isn't a Hippie."

She didn't want to talk about them anymore. Just as well. I felt lousy talking about dead Tony like that. Poor very dead Tony. What a way to go. I shivered.

Her fingers had stroked and stroked, almost absent-mindedly and the Damon miracle had reoccurred. I am always big, you understand, but now I had firmed up into something she could really use again.

"I don't believe it," she muttered in the gloom, almost to herself.

"Tut, tut. It's nothing."

"Nothing? You call that nothing!"

I rolled away from her, got up on my knees and she scrambled to get under me, her long sturdy legs widening out in a waiting V. Her eyes shone in the darkness. Her breasts tumulted again. My being flooded with new vitamins and joyful masculinity. I felt like beating my chest like Tarzan after he kayoes the lion. Or crocodile, or what have you.

"Oh, Roddddddddd. . . ." Her voice trailed off in awe.

"You said it, baby," I said in a low voice and plunged downward. My aim was uncanny. She came apart, widening to receive the delivery and her thighs immediately engulfed me. I pressed the throttle and drilled for oil. Honey. Both. She had both in huge, inexhaustible amounts. It's great to be young, willing, eager and strong. Youth always had that on its side. We old Masters in our thirties, wiser perhaps, still can't draw on the reserves and the resources of the very young. At nineteen, Adele Ash, with her build and mind and my instruction, was a super-woman.

Quite an assortment of gushers sprang up between us. In the end, geysering more slowly but with complete satisfaction, we settled down once again into two limp loving lumps of fiery flesh.

She huddled against my chest, kissing me.

"I love you," she said.

"Sure you do. Now. This minute. You should. You can't sleep like this without love being a part of it."

"No, no," she protested, "I really love you!"

"Nonsense. You'll love the very next man that makes you feel like this. Women always do. You know how many times a girl has told me she loved me? Beyond number. And all those girls are alive and well and living in a happy marriage."

"Stinker." She bit my chin and then kissed it to make it well. She was purring now, a six-foot pussycat. It was somehow incongruous but it was nice. She had driven all the fears and doubts and chicken liver out of my system. As regarded the Great Spy Hunt.

I had almost forgotten about my poor student corpses.

Almost but not quite. There's always someone or something around to bring me back to the awful earth.

The next voice I heard was that of the man I learned to loathe.

"Damn you, Damon! Exactly what I expected! Half your staff brutally murdered and you go into mourning by indulging in a sex spree! Good God, man—have you no sense of decency!"

Adele squealed and tried to hide under me and the cold wind from the front door that fanned my rump had brought in with it a roaring, insensate, really pissed-off Walrus-moustache. You were never safe when you hooked up with people like him. He somehow managed to get the keys to locked doors, ferreted you out of hiding places you holed up in and always got his man, if he was looking for you. The Northwest Mounties lost a great cop when he decided to pool his talents with the Thaddeus X. Coxe Foundation.

I climbed off Adele Ash, who then burrowed under a sheet to hide—she was still a schoolgirl after all and she had been humping in her room, which is strictly against the regulations of a university that even had a Rod Damon going for it—and reached for my pants. The man in the bowler hat, with moustache and attaché case to match, had turned on the lights in a very ungentlemanly way. He stood by the door, still glaring at me, nearly apoplectic with moral justification. Balls. I was tired and mad myself. What right had he to come busting into my love life again? Like he always did—without knocking even!

"You," I said, "are definitely not wanted here. Couldn't you phone me?"

"I have been ringing you for an hour. Then instinct and a rueful remembrance of your peccadilloes led me here. You were seen by one of the students, entering this room —a Miss Clovis Lee."

"A jealous fink." I buttoned my shirt and patted Adele Ash's twin buttocks outlined under the sheet. She had her ass up and her face down. "It's all right, honey. Don't worry. You stay where you are. I'll take this noisy prude back to my room."

Walrus-moustache exploded at that. His attaché case fell out of his hands down to the floor.

"By thunder, you are a scoundrel, Damon. With all this mad murdering going on—those poor students of yours, and it was your idea, I might add—you stoop to this. A banquet of the flesh. As God is my judge, I have lost all respect for you. You are beneath contempt!"

I saw red, blue, green and orange. What right had he to be my judge? Him! The biggest butcher of all—who played at being Spy.

"Will you stop sounding like the sound track of a Cecil

103

B. deMille movie?" I roared. "You sanctimonious bastard. I didn't kill Fat-Ass, I didn't gang-bang Rita Cortez, I didn't cut Tony Eden's whatsit off and I certainly didn't carve up Corinne Murphy with a Bowie knife—and I certainly didn't leave all those notes——"

I stopped. I could have bitten my own tongue off. Adele Ash had materialized from under the sheet, her great breasts rising and falling. Her face was as white as the sheets. Walrus-moustache, for all his anger, was stunned by the beauty of her. Adele looked at me, her red mouth and tumbling honey-colored hair awry.

Shock and agony filled her eyes. It was a helluva way to learn the awful truth.

"What's he saying, Rod? Tony—Corinne—" Rita's gang-bang hadn't really bothered anybody that much. Most of the girls had thought she had it coming to her for being so damn uppity and formal.

"Satisfied, you bastard?" I snarled at Walrus-moustache before turning back to her. "Sorry, Adele. Yes, it's true. Tony and Corinne were murdered. Him, yesterday—last night. Her, today. I didn't want to tell you. Truth is, I didn't know how——"

"And you let me make love to you all the time knowing—"

Her mouth puckered, her breasts undulated. She started to say something to me, something that Walrus-moustache would have approved of, I suppose, when the double horror hit her. Her eyelids fluttered, we saw the whites of her baby blues and then with a soft moan, letting go the sheet, she toppled in a dead faint.

In bed.

She looked like she was sleeping.

I stared at her, trying not to run across the room to smash my old friend and spy mentor in the chops. Boy, did he have it coming. But all I felt at that particular moment was a great sorrow and shame. Yes, shame. Maybe the world is right. Maybe I am a whoremaster. But does crying or the social amenities change things? Anything? Does it bring people back from the grave?

"She'll be all right," I said in a low voice. "Let her

104

sleep it off. Best thing for her. Come on. We'll go to my room."

Walrus-moustache stared at Adele Ash for a moment longer.

"Lovely thing. So blonde and fresh." His manner was like night and day now. "Sorry, Damon. I shouldn't have done this. Spouting like a spinster at you . . . I *do* apologize."

"Forget it. You can't change your bad habits. I can't change mine. That's the way the friendship crumbles."

We walked back up to my floor, after carefully closing Adele Ash's door. Walrus-moustache was contrite and silent now, he who had come roaring in like a lion. I didn't like him as a lamb so I changed the subject.

"What's new?"

"Nothing much. I have managed to keep this all quiet, as you may have noticed. I've got men checking out that bowling alley and travel agency as you mentioned in your reports. And the pier. And that posh apartment house where the Murphy girl was killed today. Nothing much, I'm afraid."

"So am I. Scared purple. What can we do?"

"Sit tight and wait. It has to end. That club, *The Alarm Clock* where Tony Eden was supposed to have gone with Murphy—it burned to the ground this morning. Strange fire. Grease on the stove or something."

"Or something." We had reached my room door. "Let's face it. I'm a bust as a spy. Get someone else before more of the kids get killed. I'm beginning to feel like Judas Iscariot."

"Nonsense, Damon. Don't let minor mishaps dampen your spirit. The Mexican traffic still very merrily goes on. We still have to stop it. It's our duty."

"Duty, schmuty. I'm thinking of those kids. Pete Porter, Adele, Norma Davis, Alice Potter. Even Rita Cortez, maybe. You want to get them all slaughtered too?"

"No, of course not. I have a plan. Care to hear it?"

We stepped into my rooms and I locked the door. He smiled at me. I smiled back. We were friends again.

For a little while, at least.

105

CHAPTER ELEVEN

With the door locked, we got cozy. I rummaged for a bottle of Johnny Walker, set up two glasses and Walrus-moustache, despite his severe-looking kisser, relaxed.

"Damon, I have a question for you."

"If it's about my love life, skip it. No more lectures. If it's about this spy-ring-around-the-rosy, let's have it."

"I come not to reproach you anymore. My word on it." He raised his glass and drained it in one gulp. I was surprised. Even he doesn't hit the sauce that way unless he's terribly impressed with something.

"Go on," I said. "This should be good."

"It is. Very well, I shall. Now, Question: how does the Enemy seem to know so much about your operation?"

"Answer: I don't know. I'm clumsy, I guess."

"Nonsense, my boy. You've done your utmost, in spite of my, ah, statements upstairs in the lady's room. She one of your flying squad, by the way?"

"She is and I don't want her getting killed."

"Precisely my point. You enlist the aid of several of your students, seven in all I believe you said, and nobody else knows what is going on. So how can they all be killed like this—especially as harmless looking as they are and how much could they have known that would have led someone to kill them in such a ghastly manner? Also it's inconceivable that four of them—the fat one, the man and the other two ladies should all have tumbled onto something important enough, all in *different* parts of town, that would force the Enemy to kill them. Are you following me?"

"Yes, I think I am. And I don't want to. You're not trying to tell me that——"

"Exactly. There's a traitor in your midst. A double agent. And for all your codes and passwords, you've played right into the hands of our enemies. It's the only possible answer for this blood bath."

"You're guessing or you've got proof. Which is it?" My

106

mind boggled at what he was saying. One of the kids a traitor—Pete Porter, Rita Cortez, Adele Ash, Norma Davis, *Alice Potter?* It wasn't really possible.

"Proof," he said, sourly, reaching into his inner coat pocket for something. "But our traitor must be a man, you understand. Because all of the women were brutally assaulted sexually as well as murdered."

"Hold on, this *Glee Club* is a bunch of gang-bangers. Men and women. Remember the notes and remember what I told you about the night I bailed out Rita Cortez. That wasn't one man, that was an army."

"Well, let's put it this way. Miss Cortez was not killed. It is entirely possible that is the one isolated case in all these assaults. From what you've told me about Miss Cortez, she very well could have merely run into a bunch of wild boys——"

"Maybe, but I don't think so. It has to be the same bunch. And what's that you're holding in your hand. The proof?"

He was holding a small roll of something in his hand that looked like microfilm. It was no longer than the stub of a cigarette. His smile was deadly calm. He was sure he knew what he was talking about. I waited for him to go on.

"Our men in Frisco tracked down a woman agent to a bar on Fisherman's Wharf. Quite a catch. The lady was Marlene Rakovny, a very dangerous Russian agent. She chose to shoot it out with our agents rather than be taken alive. Miss Rakovny was forty-two and quite sexy. She didn't want to spend the rest of her life in a Federal penitentiary. You would have liked her, Damon. Your sort of woman."

"I'll bet. Go on."

"She tried to proposition the agent whose lap she lay in even as her life flowed out of five bullet holes. Dying, she told him that the Chinese Red tide would sweep over America—her exact words—and that she only regretted that she would die without meeting the great Rod Damon face to face. That was when she asked the agent to make love to her. She died in his arms while he pretended to agree. It was then that he heard her say—and again I am

107

quoting exactly—'*poor Damon. Working with a double-agent hanging around his neck. . . .*'"

"You're sure she said that. No mistake?"

"It's an exact quote."

"Maybe she was lying."

"Persons a few breaths from dying seldom do. I chose to take the word of a dying woman in this case. Even a notorious spy."

"Dammit, it's so hard to swallow. And what's on that precious microfilm? A picture of me as a baby on a bear-skin rug, measurements and all?"

He shook his head, his manner more serious than ever.

"No, it is a copy of sealed orders to Miss Rakovny advising her where to go and who to see to arrange the transport of some fifty more agents into this country. We found it in a false pocket of her brassiere. Thanks to catching her, we have been able to stop fifty agents from leaking into the country."

"Then why aren't you satisfied? Geezis, fifty spies. That's a lot of red herring, isn't it?"

"A lot, yes. But we're greedy at the Foundation. We want more. We want all of them. We have to put a stop to this. Why do the Chinese want so many operatives in this country? Do you know? We don't. And there's the rub. We can't stop until we put an end to all this!"

"Cool off. I get the point. Want some more hootch?"

"Please, yes." He tucked the microfilm in a side pocket and handed me his glass. I refilled it. While I was passing the glass back to him, my phone rang. We looked at each other and then at it. Then we looked at each other again.

"Answer it," he ordered. "And hope for the best."

"You say. Everything's been going crazy lately—" I swept the receiver to my ear.

"Damon, here."

"*When the weather's hot and sticky, that's no time to dunk the dicky,*" a voice said with a sibilant whisper I couldn't recognize. I froze. Only myself and the kids knew that code. Unless—

"Who is this?" I rasped.

The voice took a beat and then answered.

108

"Help, there are sharks in these waters."

"Dammit, say what you have to say or get off the line!" My temples were bursting.

"Very well," the voice continued. "Go to Ferry Park. Just beneath the statue of Washington crossing the Delaware. Some of your friends will be there, waiting for you."

Before I could figure out if it was a man's voice or a woman's, the bastard hung up. I ran to the closet for my coat and Walrus-moustache moved to block me. His grim face was grimmer than ever, and his moustaches twitched.

"What was that all about?"

"Strange voice using the code I gave my students. Sounds bad. Trouble all the way. Ferry Park. I have to get out there and you can't stop me—"

"I'll go with you."

"No. You stay here. Keep an eye on Adele Ash and the rest of them if they're in the building. You know their names." I shuddered. "I got a feeling I'm not going to like what I find under the statue of Washington crossing the Delaware. Goddamn those Glee Club bastards!"

"Damon, what *are* you talking about?"

"Stay put," I growled. "I'll call you as soon as I find out what gives." He didn't try to stop me. He nodded and twisted the droop of his moustache.

"You be careful. I can't afford to lose you. Not now."

"Got a gun?"

He nodded again, opened his attaché case and handed over a .32 calibre pistol. His eyes were almost sad. He was fond of me, like I told you. I might have been his own horny son.

As I raced down the corridor, I tried to keep my mind off what I might find at the base of the statue in Ferry Park. It was a Lover's Lane section, well-used and famous among the students of the university. Not for the usual historical reasons. There were lots of trees, as many bushes and the cops left it strictly alone.

Damn the luck.

It would be a perfect place for the Glee Club or whoever was responsible for this whole mess, to operate in.

As it turned out, it was.

109

I found Alice Potter and Norma Davis just at the very foot of the Washington statue. It was already a moonlight night and even before I dug my flashlight out of the glove compartment of the Renault, I could see what had happened to them wasn't nice at all. In life, they had liked to run around together, being sort of look-alikes as they were. Both young, both blonde, both knockouts. In death, they resembled each other even more. The mad fiends who had been wrecking and destroying my secret group had gone on another murderous, hellish spree.

Alice was minus her left breast and Norma *still* looked like her. Only her left breast was intact; it was *her* right one that was missing. And to add to the gory picture, both ladies were lying together on the stone cold ground in a Red Sea of their own blood. I clicked the flashlight off. There wasn't anything to see anymore. The dark trees and bushes of Ferry Park could have held a million assassins. Something in me was dead; I've never felt like that before. When the young and beautiful die so needlessly with a lifetime of living and loving ahead of them, then the whole world was crazy.

It sure was.

There were no notes from the Glee Club this time; not so much as a chalk mark on the flagstones beneath the naked corpses of the girls. I looked up at General George's statue. Silhouetted against the moonlit sky, I saw a pair of men's legs sticking up into the air. I jumped. But the legs weren't moving. Deep doom hit me; it had to be Pete Porter, the last man among the group. With a shaking hand and leg, I boosted myself up to take a look.

I got a jolt.

Washington and two stone figures had been mocked up in the prow of a boat. Between the stone sides of this craft, the man's legs were upthrust. In the flashlight glare, I saw that it wasn't Peter Porter. It was a stranger.

A small, nondescript man in ordinary suit and uncommon knife sticking out of his heart. The face was broad, Slavic. Almost fascinated by this switch, I examined his clothes and his possessions.

As cool as the night was, I was on fire. With rage,

110

terror and discovery. When I found what I was looking for, I turned the flash off again and thought for a long time. In the dark, I might have been crossing the Delaware with General George.

There were enough papers and documents and things on the dead man to label him for what he was. One Maxim Koloksky, Russian agent and Communist card holder, belonging to a cell. It was ridiculous, all around, to say the least. Not only were the Chinese Reds knocking off my people and sending spies into the country, they were also murdering and delivering Russian secret agents!

I was perplexed, baffled and bewildered.

And sick again.

Visions of Norma Davis and Alice Potter, one-breasted into an early grave, had my stomach doing flip-flops and handsprings. What the hell was I going to do now?

Then I heard the running feet of a man. Coming toward me and the statue. I tensed, peering over the stone side of the boat. There was a big heavy shadow darting for where the girls lay. It was a big man. His feet were thundering on the flagstones.

I don't know where my courage came from. I vaulted over the rim of the statue and landed smack in front of him. Between him and the two quiet corpses which shone dully in the moonlight. I flung out a fist, the one with the flashlight in it and the man dodged, cursed and tried to tackle me. It was then, and only then, that I saw it was Pete Porter.

Coming around me, he saw the girls first. He stopped dead in his tracks and as dark as it was, I could see the blood drain out of his face. Then he spotted me and his face crumpled. I grabbed his arm.

"Pete—for God's sakes—what the hell were you doing?"

"Professor, I—did you—are they—oh, hell!" He punched his big hands together and the smacking noise made my ears ache.

"Don't look at them," I warned him. "Yes, it's Norma and Alice. You want to have nightmares the rest of your

111

life? They're both dead and I want to know why you came running up to them like that?"

He shuddered, he was sobbing openly, his big body trembling like jello on the plate.

"We had an idea, me and the girls. I went along with it, seeing as how we were getting nowhere with this operation. They made a date with two sunburned characters at the big department store in town. You know—Neeley's? So I said, you go along with the gag and I'll shadow you. Only thing was—somebody put a hole in my gas tank. I've been running from about three miles back. I couldn't get a lift—goddamn it, but *nobody* gave me a lift!"

"The world is afraid of hitchhikers. Forget it for now. These men from Neeley's. They work there or just customers?"

"Customers. The girls ran into them in the sporting goods section. I never got a close look at them. Just the sunburns. Goddamnit, Prof, who put that hole in my tank? Why was I late? Why couldn't I get a lift? In the name of God——"

"Shut up. Don't fold now. If I had the answers to those questions, I wouldn't have to screw for a living. Sit down and take it easy. We have to think. Think hard."

There was a bench nearby. We sat down. I took one of his cigarettes that he offered me and we both lit up. Smoking has its beneficial aspects; this was only one of them. When you're holding a wake over the dead, it helps.

"God," he whimpered again. "Just too late—"

"Too late for tears too," I said.

"Doreen, Tony, Corinne, Alice, Norma—" He shook his head. "What is the world coming to?"

I didn't remind him about Rita Cortez. After all, she hadn't been killed. In his book, a gang-bang couldn't have been all that bad. I know how he felt.

The living have nothing to complain about, as long as they aren't dead. Right?

"How did you know about Tony and Corinne?" I asked mildly enough. "It wasn't exactly general knowledge and I didn't put it on the P.A. system back at the university."

He didn't read anything into my question.

112

"I stopped by the police station this afternoon. That cop Johnson told me. I went off my rocker. When I spotted Alice and Norma doing that department store routine, I went along with it. I didn't tell them either. Figured it would scare them silly. Maybe I should have. Now, I don't know."

"Me, neither," I agreed. "What we do now is report this to the cops, go on back home and try to keep ourselves from getting chopped up. This has gone far enough. I'm pulling the rest of you kids off this. Let the FBI and the CIA handle this. I had no business trying to make spies of you. It's my fault, really."

"You can't!" He glared at me wildly, the cigarette jutting from his strong mouth. "We gotta get even! We gotta pay these rats back. Every single blamed one of them! You ought to put the whole school in on this play! Nobody kills one of us and gets away with it!"

"That's very commendable, Pete, but you're upset. You don't know what you're saying. You went to the university to learn about Sex, not to get your nuts chopped up."

His face got as cold as a lamb chop in deep freeze.

"Maybe," he said, "but not anymore. You got to see it that way too, Prof."

"Yeah. I gotta. Maybe you're right. Come on. I'll cover the girls with my coat and we'll take the Renault down to Headquarters. Johnson just isn't going to believe this. He may lock me up for life. You too. There's a dead Russian spy with George up there and—"

"Screw Johnson. He's only a cop. He'll have to believe us—what dead spy?"

Famous last words.

Johnson not only didn't believe us, he locked us up, had us examined by police psychiatrists and then threw the key away. And we didn't get a chance to call our lawyers or make one phone call.

Unconstitutional, but that's how it worked out.

Pete Porter and I spent the night in jail. In separate cells while the spy killers ran around loose.

I couldn't even get a message to Walrus-moustache.

113

Like Johnson said:

"—maybe you're innocent and maybe you're not, but five college kids have been butchered by some local Jack the Ripper or Rippers and I'm not going to take any more chances. This case has been dumped in my lap since the fat gal got hers, and by Judas Priest, there aren't going to be any more murders tonight! I need my sleep. With you in jail, Professor, and your pal there, maybe I can get it. We'll just see, huh?"

A cop is a cop is a cop.

And who could blame him?

Cops like to give out tickets for jaywalking, arrest harmless drunks, assist lovely old ladies across the street and pat schoolchildren on the head. None of them want to mix with gangsters, buck to politicians and least of all do they like to go tiptoeing through the corpses. It makes good reading but most bulls like things nice and quiet.

I had to go along with Johnson. I think I would have locked me and Pete Porter up too. We could have been very dangerous characters. You couldn't blame Johnson for not wanting to take any more chances.

"Jeepers," Pete Porter roared, tugging at the iron bars of his cell. "How the hell are we going to accomplish anything in here?"

"Take it easy, Pete," I sympathized. "My friend will get us out of here by morning. You'll see."

"What friend?" he ripped back sarcastically. "J. Edgar Hoover?"

"Nope. Not him. J. Edgar Walrus-moustache."

"Huh?" Pete Porter's eyes bugged out.

I didn't bother explaining. Porter was upset enough for two college boys fighting for the same spot on the football squad.

But I was wrong about old Walrus-moustache. When another sun dawned over the university, he was in more hot water than I was. The way it turned out, he would need a pretty damn good lawyer himself.

Somebody like Clarence Darrow and Sam Leibowitz and Louis Nizer all rolled into one.

114

But I didn't know that as I watched the cockroaches walk across the ceiling of my cell.

I was too stunned by what was happening to my kids to think.

CHAPTER TWELVE

Walrus-moustache got the hots for Adele Ash. It was as simple as that. Underneath that bowler hat beat the heart of a whoremaster, as I had always known. And the whoremaster emerged whenever the old goat got his chance. His chance being with me in lock-up and him keeping a weather eye on Adele Ash. I can just imagine what sight of that six-foot charmer did to the pulses of a sneaky horn-toad like Walrus-moustache.

When Johnson gave me the details the next morning, it was about ten o'clock. Poor Johnson. He had aged fifty years since the last time I saw him. I couldn't blame him. He had another messy pair of corpses on his hands.

I saw Johnson in private. He had me delivered in hand-cuffs to his private office while Pete Porter chewed the bars of his cell in anger. I didn't know what Johnson was up to until he told me all about Walrus-moustache. And Adele Ash.

It was a rotten little horrible yarn and as I listened, I felt like I was going crazy. Johnson's neat dark hair was all tousled and irregular as if he had been pulling out handfuls of the stuff. His eyes were bloodshot and he was breathing funny. For one screwy second, I thought he was going to strangle me with his bare hands. But he then quieted down and walked to the barred window and looked out. His back was to me but he started talking. He talked a long time. I didn't have the strength or the brains to interrupt to ask questions. I let him go oh talking.

What he told me was as screwy as the rest of the case had been and was.

Another jump into the laughing academy.

A pipeline to the nuthouse.

I was going out of my head, forgetting all about Sex

115

and things, in a crazy spy caper that had everything to do with Sex so far. Abnormal Sex, that is. Spies? A gang of sex-crazy killers were running amuck!

What had happened to Walrus-moustache and Adele Ash shouldn't have happened to dogs. To two screwing dogs.

From what Johnson told me, and what he had been able to piece together, this is what happened after I took off for Ferry Park. Right after:

Walrus-moustache had gone upstairs to talk to Adele Ash. He must have talked real fine (and being the kind of man he is) didn't want to hanky-panky Adele Ash on the university grounds proper. Like lay her in her own room, et cetera. So he got her to leave the university with him and together they rode off into the sunset toward the *Drop Inn Motel* right on the intersection of the highway leading out of the city.

Maybe Walrus-moustache had another hot tip, besides his own. Who knows? Anyway, Adele went with him and they signed the register at the *Drop Inn* as Mr. and Mrs. Damon. (Damn his hide!) Now, they stay there for about three long hours, all the time I'm in the park with Pete Porter and then getting locked up by Johnson and Company. Nothing harmful so far. The old goat chasing a bunny and having some laughs. Why not? Taking his mind off his troubles. Great.

Then the owner of the motel, a fat, huffy character named Joseph de Oregano, told Johnson that about midnight or so, he heard some funny sounds from Cabin Number Nine. Like a woman in trouble and then a man yelling some crazy thing like *"It's a girl! It's a girl! I knew it!"* This Oregano character had thought that Walrus-moustache did kind of look like a doctor (now he was convinced) and that Adele Ash could have been pregnant—how can you ever tell with really big girls who wear shifts? So he runs down to Cabin Number Nine, expecting to be handed a cigar or at the very least to charge his customers for three registrations instead of two. Oregano is a real sweetheart, you see.

What he is handed when he barges in on Number Nine

116

is a case of the heebie-jeebies, the galloping shudders and nightmares to last him for the rest of his natural life. Later when Johnson pumped him dry with questions, Oregano claimed he heard no car drive off (or up) during the course of all the trouble.

This was the part of Johnson's story that was hardest for me to take. What Mr. Oregano found in Cabin Number Nine. I tried not to throw up again. Never mind how bad and sorry I felt for the dead (there are times when you just can't think of them and this was one of them), I didn't want to go chicken-liver in front of Johnson.

There were three people in the cabin. Two men and one woman. Two of the people were dead. Horribly dead. And the third one was in pretty sad-assed shape. Him I really felt sorry for.

The Glee Club, for I refused to think it was anyone else, had taken Adele Ash, with all that loveliness and youth and hot body, and spread-eagled her on the big double bed in the room. Each foot and each hand was lashed to one of the posters. Adele was naked, naturally, for what maniac ever leaves the clothes on his victim?

Her eyes were wide open when Johnson finally got there after Oregano worked up enough guts to phone. The blue eyes were stark, staring mad. No wonder. They (or he or she) had taken a sharp instrument of some kind, maybe the Bowie knife again, and played a game of Tic-Tac-Toe across her lovely torso. The X's had won and the winning slash was a vicious line ending in her heart with a gaping wound. There was no weapon on the premises. From the Medical Examiner's on the spot autopsy, Adele had been assaulted sexually numberless times. That couldn't have been Walrus-moustache! He's a romantic from the Old School, as horny as he is.

The rest of it was just as baffling.

There was a dead man in the bathroom, knifed through the heart, and from all indications a repeat character on the one I had found in Washington's stone boat. Another Ivan type, complete with Slavic face, ID cards and just as dead. The Enemy was still depositing dead red herrings all over the case.

Walrus-moustache?

Worst of all, when you consider what he was up against.

He was found under the bed, with a wallop on the sconce that would have killed a lesser man. Right now he was in the hospital in a coma and nobody could say if he would ever come out of it. The old hard head that usually wore a bowler was now swathed in bandages from pate to shoulders.

All I could think of while Johnson was slowly giving me the gruesome details was the sentence and the words that Joseph de Oregano claimed to have heard: *"It's a girl! It's a girl—"*

If Walrus-moustache had shouted that, what did he mean? Did he mean what I thought he meant? What we had been discussing in my rooms only last night?

Again, there were no notes from the Glee Club murderer-fiends. Not unless you consider playing Tic-Tac-Toe on a girl's body some kind of message.

I could taste my prison breakfast. My mouth was bile. I breathed deeply and the sensation left for a little while.

Johnson turned from the window. Even the recital of what he had already known left another mark on his face. He looked as pathetic as a spinster when the last man on earth takes off for the moon and she can't go.

"Well, Damon?"

"Well, what? I've been here all night, remember? Under lock and key. And I don't like Tic-Tac-Toe. And I don't kill beautiful girls like Adele Ash. I lay them."

His teeth showed. "Smarty. What the hell is that university of yours? A gathering place for sex fiends? In all my years as a policeman—you know the spot you put me in?"

"For instance?" Him talking about spots. What was I —in green fields of clover?

"I'll have to give this to the press now. This is an epidemic. Six college students brutally assaulted and murdered. Two dead Russian spies. I gave it over the teletype already. The FBI and the CIA and God knows what else will be crawling all over this place this afternoon. I'd like to be able to answer some of their questions."

"Me too."

"Then answer some of mine."

"I'll try."

He came over to my chair and firmly glared down at me.

"What do you do exactly at that university?"

"I'm a sexologist. The titular head of L.S.D."

"What's a sexologist? And what's L.S.D.—as though I don't know."

"You don't. I study Sex, that's all you need to know. And the initials L.S.D. stands for League of Sexual Dynamics."

"Geezis, I knew it! Sex! Is that why all these kids are getting chopped up like this—some screwy kind of sex research?"

"Of course not. Figure it out for yourself, Johnson. I'm a believer in Love not Hate."

"Sure, sure. And I'm Onassis. Listen, who is the character with the moustache we found under the bed?"

"Walrus-moustache? He's connected with the Thaddeus X. Coxe Foundation. A society devoted to peace. They pay for my grant that enables me to work at the university."

He pulled out some more of his hair with both hands.

"Don't double-talk me, Damon. I've got seven stiffs in the police morgue—no, eight. I could make you nine or put you under the third degree without batting an eye."

I looked up at him. I maintained a calm I did not feel.

"Hear me out, Johnson. You look like an intelligent man."

"I'm listening."

"I want to make a deal."

His eyes glowed. "You'll confess then?" He reached for a pencil and paper.

"No, I won't confess. I'm clean. I want to make a deal."

"Go on. Make it good."

"Turn me loose. Give me until ten o'clock tonight. I think I can wrap this up for you."

He laughed, then he sneered and then he laughed again.

"Judas Priest, just like in the movies on television. The

119

hero is caught, he tells the cops he'll wrap it up, and what do you know, at ten o'clock on the nose he solves everything! What am I—an idiot? You know anything, you tell me now. I don't want to find your body at ten o'clock with a knife sticking up your you-know-what."

"Ahah! Then you agree I couldn't possibly have had anything to do with what happened in Cabin Number Nine last night?"

"How could you?" he growled defeatedly. "You were here, locked up and you ain't Houdini. No, I thought about that. But you're mixed up in this, all right. All the way. That I'm positive of. So what can you sell me that I'll buy?"

"The solution to all these murders."

"Go on."

"You want to be able to show those city slickers from D.C. that you're not just a hick cop, don't you? Well, I can help you."

His eyes narrowed. Suspicious, shifty. He didn't trust me.

"In a word—how?"

"Let me walk out of here. Put a tail on me if you like. I have to go back to the university. Maybe the answer's there."

"What answer?"

I couldn't tell him about the Red Chinese or the Foundation's real job or what I had to do for a living sometimes. The code of the Bonds, and all that crap. But I did have a lead. A good one. I wasn't kidding him about that.

"Back at the university is the key to all this. Someone there knows about all these crimes. It's an inside job. It has to be. There are some leads I'd like to check out. *I* have to do it. You can't. You're a cop. Nobody will talk to you knowing that. You see?"

"I see, all right. Maybe you want to take a powder, catch a jet to Alaska——"

"No, no, no. Put a tail on me like I said. A good one. I won't shake him. I just want to go on about my business."

"I don't know." He was hedging.

120

"Know," I persisted. "Those big city boys will be here this afternoon. Remember?"

He thought about it for a full minute. His haggard face looked twice as lined and worried. Then with a sudden growl of decision, he dug into his back pocket, fished out some keys and undid the manacles that bound my wrists.

"I'm crazy," he said. "But I'll gamble."

"Good for you. You won't regret this."

"What about your friend? The kid, Porter?"

"Leave him where he is. He's safer here."

"Wouldn't you be?" he asked meaningfully. His eyes glittered at me. I shook off a shudder.

"You said it all. Six of my students have been killed. Okay. I don't want any more of them hurt. I'll watch my own ass. You can bet on that."

"You bet your ass you will," he said sourly. "And no tricks. You show up at ten o'clock with your riddle solved or you'll really find out just how tough this hick cop can be."

"I promise."

"On what?"

"I was an Eagle Scout once—want my oath?"

"Go on, get going." He reached down again, pressed a buzzer on the squawk-box on his desk and muttered some instructions into it. He clicked it off and I was on my way out the door. He had one last reminder for me as I walked out of his life—temporarily.

"Oh, Professor?"

"Yes, Johnson?"

"Good luck. See you at ten o'clock."

I didn't like the way he said it. It had funeral wreaths and sympathy cards all over it. I shuddered again. Everybody was hanging crepe all over me. But I kept on going, right out of that damn police station to where the Renault was still parked in the driveway. They hadn't put it in the police garage, like they do with bad vehicles involved in misdemeanors, felonies and homicides.

I wondered if Walrus-moustache would pull out of his coma. Pull out of everything. I hoped fervently that he and Adele Ash had gotten some fun out of life before

121

she lost hers. Poor Adele. What a waste of woman-flesh. What a waste of all of them. Dear big Fat Ass, Corinne Murphy, Alice Potter, Norma Davis. Not to mention Tony Eden. AC or DC, he must have pleasured a lot of people. As for Rita Cortez, the gang-bang that had almost wrecked her forever—as bad as it might have been—at least she could still smell the pretty perfumes.

Clovis Lee.

She'd been out of it. All of it. The whole thing. If I had rung her into the assignment, the chances were good that she would be pushing up daisies now instead of pushing me off her stomach. I had a twinge of nostalgia, recalling her delightful body, as I put the Renault in gear. I hadn't been snowing Johnson. I did have an idea. And it had everything to do with Walrus-moustache's blurted exclamation. It had to be him who shouted something about knowing it and knowing it was a *girl*. The remark only made sense when I linked it with our conversation about the dying statement of sexy Marlene Rakovny, the shoot-out in Frisco and all the dope about a traitor in my midst. An albatross hung around my neck from the word go.

A traitor.

A *woman*.

But how could that be when all the murders and killings marked the work of a perverted man or men? The Glee Club could be just minions, of course, but how could I be sure of that? Most traitors like to work alone. Maybe Walrus-moustache was right. Except for the plural signature, maybe the attack on Rita Cortez *was* an isolated thing that had nothing to do with the overall trouble. Maybe—roosters don't crow.

I eased the Renault out toward the thoroughfare, finding light traffic and giving Johnson's unseen tail enough time to pin himself on my rear. I nosed the car toward the university to the east. It was a sunny day. Big Sol was bathing the land with an orange glow and it would have been hard to believe he was smiling down on so much killing.

So much blood.

122

So much utter waste.

When I thought about the dead girls, I wanted to scream, kick my windshield out and chew metal. So I didn't think about them. It was easier that way. Made more sense too. Why clutter up what brain I had with remorse, regrets and might-have-beens?

So I thought about the traitor.

Thought about Pete Porter in jail.

Clovis Lee flitting in and out of my bedroom and my life, willy-nilly.

And the untouchable, so far, Miss Rita Cortez.

Well, her time had come.

She was either going to have to screw or get off the team.

Walrus-moustache had to be wrong, though.

The traitor *must* be a man. It had to be a man. A master spy or killer would have been the one to put his mark on Doreen, Corinne, Alice, Norma and Adele. Psychotically, it fit. The killer's ego would have *demanded* it! If I were nuts like that, that's the way I would have done it.

In a fog of confusion, I drove back to the university nestling in the green hills of Paradise. And Sudden Death.

As confused as I was, though, I remembered several interesting things. Like several points in Aragoli's thesis on *How To Bring The Pristine Woman You Want, To Heel*. The ancient Spanish sexologist, still alive and living it up in Castro's Cuba, had a lousy set of political beliefs but he still was an ace in matters of Sex.

Even as I tooled the Renault toward home, seventy-five-year-old Aragoli's historic tome, which was still in print since it rolled off a two-bit printing press in Seville in 1928, was practically the Bible on the subject.

To wit:

Aragoli's three main points were—when dealing with a potential hold-out like the Rita Cortez's of this world, were these:

A. Don't give her a chance to make up her mind. If the time and the place and the setting is right, upend her on the nearest piece of available space, (furniture, rug or floor) and hop to it.

123

_____*B.* Do not stop what you are doing no matter how she screams, claws or protests that she is not that sort of woman.

C. Above all, and the most important point of all, be sure that she climaxes. *One way or another,* no matter what you have to do to bring her to that point.

Good old brutal Aragoli.

A bit hard perhaps, slightly harsh and even a mite animalistic, but—the technique was guaranteed for the true bull of a man.

And I intended to follow all three of the doughty Spaniard's precepts in the matter of Rita Cortez.

Aha, Toro!

CHAPTER THIRTEEN

"You wanted to see me, Professor Damon?"

"You bet. Come on in and shut the door. I want to talk to you."

"Certainly. I'm always glad to talk to you."

Rita Cortez ambled into my rooms. With all of that slow, tigerish, hips-timed-to-a-jungle-ecstasy rhythm of hers. She looked absolutely gorgeous. The ordeal of the bowling alley seemed like something that had happened to three other girls. Her inky black long hair, pale ivory skin and blood-red lips were as Snow Whitish as ever. But I was feeling like Doc, not Dopey. I couldn't let the lust beacons shine out of my eyes. This was one broad I wanted!

Especially after all that had happened. My quandary came equipped with a throbbing desire that could have passed for a third leg. Or arm.

She was wearing a two-piece dress with exposed midriff. The material shimmered like silk and the skirt was banded like a Spanish dancer's. You could barely see the upper half of her navel. And there ought to be a law about navels like that one. I had a mad desire to fill it.

She sauntered to the center of the room, all her goodies seeming to twirl. Her green eyes flickered.

124

"What do you want me to do?" she purred.

"Who says I want you to do something?"

"Don't you?" She smiled and her lidded eyes glanced at the open bedroom door. "I am ready, you know. We have waited rather long enough. I no longer have the Flu, I am recovered from what those—ah, people—did to me—and wasn't it yourself who always said that when it comes to Sex, there's no time like the present?"

"Stop reading my mind," I said gruffly. "I do plan that, yes. But first we have to have a talk."

"All right. But it really isn't necessary. After all, you are the great Professor Damon."

"Let me be the judge of that. Now sit down in that chair there while we talk. And stop swinging those goodies of yours. You're distracting me from what I want to say."

"I? I'm flattered." She laughed softly but she sat down. Sitting down only served to put the delectables in even more appropriate focus. Her crossed legs, taper of hip and bulging bodice would have ruined the best intentions of an army of do-gooders.

I assumed my most professorial air. I folded my arms again.

"Good. Now let's begin at the beginning. You *do* know what's been going on lately?"

"You mean the girls and poor Tony Eden—yes, I know. How could I not know?"

I wondered how good the university grapevine really was. Since I had called her in kind of late on the Spy squad and things had been kept hush-hush, it was hard to know if the old college was in a panic. She couldn't know yet about Adele Ash and Walrus-moustache and I didn't think the grapevine had gotten wind of what had happened to Alice Potter and Norma Davis. But I was past playing games with her. Direct action was the ticket now. Still, I had to sound her out first.

"All right. Then I want you to be sure what you're getting into. I want you and me to get together more than you'll ever know. But I want to do it my way in a special manner I've worked out."

Her raven black eyebrows rose. Her eyes glinted.

"You know all. I'll try any method you like. I'm especially interested in what you can show me and do to me with the old Arabian gambits. Such as Jalal al-Din al Siyuti. I've read so many of your references to him——"

"Time. You don't understand. Oh, I'll show you everything in due time, never fear. What I mean is I want you to come with me to some spot away from here. I'll admit these very rooms are most convenient for any sexual research we might want to undertake. But I'm anxious to do something about these killings. So—I want us to be seen leaving the University, getting into my car and taking off. I'm setting us up as decoys. I *think*."

"Decoys for what?"

I stared her down. She stared right back at me.

"Don't you see? Every person that's been in this spy setup with me has been harmed. Whoever is doing all these terrible things, is out to get all of us. So I'm tired of sitting around waiting for the blow to fall. So let's go for an old-fashioned ride and try to flush them out."

"But how?"

"By sticking our necks out. We'll go to the remotest place I can think of. Seemingly defenseless and all by ourselves. Out for a little woo-pitching. But don't worry. I've got a gun. I think they'll take a crack at us if they see we're unprotected and damn far from the madding crowd."

"They?"

"Sure. Got to be more than one. Didn't a whole gang of them abuse you at that bowling alley?"

"Oh." She shuddered and the tremor made both her breasts stand out some more. "I'm afraid—"

"So am I. But are you game? After all, we will at least be doing what comes naturally, in case they do go for us . . ."

The prospect seemed to thrill her. She wet her lower lip with her pink tongue.

"Where is this remote place you picked?"

I nodded.

"The university owns a mansion out on the Parkins Road. It was left as a bequest by some eccentric million-

126

aire. Big, rambling dump with stone turrets, iron picket gate and fence all around the property. It's empty because the university hasn't quite made up its mind what to do with it. Probably sell it for cash and throw it in the treasury. But it's got about twenty bedrooms and I have the key."

"You have the key." She arched her back restlessly, stirred her legs and stood up. "Then what are we waiting for? You've *talked* a good one for weeks now, Rod Damon, let's see if you can play one!"

"That's the way I like to hear my women talk. Shall I prepare a picnic basket?"

"No," she said. "I have found food a great deterrent when the main hunger is sexual desire. I don't want any other sensation to interfere."

I shook my head. "How did a doll like you ever become a call girl? With that kind of correct attitude, it must have been hell for you."

"A woman has to eat," she said simply.

I shrugged. "Anyhow, thanks for the guts to go and I'll thank you more appropriately when we get down to cases. We don't need a pass. You're with me and they kinda give me a free run around here, you know."

"Yes," she laughed. "With hot and cold running coeds. You are a devil, Damon."

"On the side of the angels. Come." I held out my hand and brought her close to me. We kissed. One long, lingering, promising buss that held out a lot of hope for a grand spree in the sheets. I was glad. It would take my mind off Walrus-moustache and the whole damn mess. And if we did flush out any spies, what the hell. Johnson's tailing car would be a big help. Meanwhile it was nice to have Walrus-moustache's .32 calibre special in my hip pocket.

My own gun is quick. But I can't stop a man with murder on his mind with it. A woman, yes—*maybe*.

Rita Cortez seemed as anxious as I was to get going so we locked up and scrammed down the corridor. I had decided to walk out the front of the building in broad daylight so we couldn't be missed. A good idea. It was sunny outside and warm and as bright as a lighted TV studio, but unfortunately we ran into Clovis Lee.

Sweet, gorgeous, jealous Clovis Lee.

When she saw the Puerto Rican bombshell on my left arm, her mouth drooped and her eyes shot sparks.

"Well, well, well," she purred icily.

"Hello, Clovis," Rita Cortez said politely.

"Hi, kid," I said airily.

Clovis looked ginger-peachy in culottes and sweater with a crimson scarf wrapped around her slim throat. But the look in her eyes was ugly. Her red hair was flaming.

"Going someplace?" she asked, ignoring Rita and giving me the Double O that said Drop Dead.

"You'll never believe this, Clovis, but Miss Cortez and I are going to officiate at a Bird Watcher's Outing in Ferry Park."

"Really? Lovebirds, I'll bet."

Nobody owns me, of course, but can I help it if women sometimes think they do? And jealousy and being catty is something I have no control over. What man has?

Rita Cortez accepted the challenge. She smiled sweetly at Clovis, took my arm more firmly and said: "I've always wanted to see a yellow-bellied sapsucker make love to a sparrow. Haven't you, Clovis?"

On that bitchy *bon mot,* I fled with Rita Cortez through the glass doors. Several passing students, fetching in shorts and school sweaters, giggled out loud, because they overheard the remark. Clovis Lee just stood her ground, frozen to the spot and two dabs of red that matched the crimson of her scarf, set her face on fire.

"You—you—*call girl!*" she hooted.

What a comeback.

We fled down the stone steps to my waiting Renault.

Across the parking area, I could see a dark sedan with no university sticker in the windows, suddenly pull out, motor going. Johnson's man. That was good. I didn't really want to wander out to a desolate place like Parkins Road without some police protection. After all, what if

128

we really ran into the Glee Club? The idea made me shiver.

In the Renault, our knees touched and Rita Cortez, rubbing it in, just in case Clovis Lee was watching, rested her head on my shoulder. Her breasts mashed me, pleasantly.

"Please, not while I'm driving."

"Oh, pooh. You can do anything."

"Can I?"

"Well—" she admitted. "I hope so. Or else you've led me on so shamelessly."

"Me?" I nosed the car out, giving Johnson's tail more time before I zipped for the long, curving macadam lane bordered by tall pines that fronted the university. "You used the seventh method on me. It wasn't the other way around. Tell me—did you really learn about it the way you said. From one of your customers?"

She took a moment before answering. The breeze was whipping her face, fanning her inky black hair beautifully.

"Don't you believe me?"

"Sure."

"No you don't. I can tell by your tone. You think I made it up."

"Did you?"

"No."

"Then why argue. I believe you."

"That's better."

We were both sounding like refugees from a Hemingway novel so I concentrated on my driving. The highway that runs by the university bears south to Parkins Road, but you have to navigate about five or six miles of hills and dales to get there. It was a lovely day for a drive. A great day to get laid.

Suddenly Rita Cortez's hand was at my crotch, the zipper unzippering before I could stop her. Her cool slender fingers had me kind of trapped. She didn't squeeze or grab. Merely fondled and caressed.

"Hey. No fair."

"Why not?"

"I'm over-prepared already. I've got a picture of you in my mind, Rita—"

"Then develop it. Little by little."

"Are you kidding?"

"Now who doesn't believe who? Go ahead. Be my guest. I've got enough Kleenex to accommodate a prep school for boys."

I flung her a look. Her lovely profile was chiseled, determined and almost as cool as a cucumber. Only a slight flush betrayed her inner restlessness. But I was suspicious as all hell now. I bit my lip.

"Care to tell me what's bothering you, Rod? You seem annoyed. Angry, almost."

"Not exactly. Can't you wait? It's only about fifteen minutes to the mansion. There's more room there. Lots of big beds. We can go around in circles for hours."

"Why should it bother you?" she said softly, her hands still making me grow bigger and bigger until I bulged. "Aren't you the great Damon? The tireless one. The one who can't get enough. I have heard that you can have a dozen orgasms and still want more. Can't I test the theory?"

"So test. But I warn you. I don't come easy."

"Yes, I know. I remember. That's what's so wonderful about you, Rod, and it's the one thing that can make a woman like me desire you all the more. Let me be a tease."

"So tease. Enjoy, enjoy."

"Doesn't it feel nice?"

"Nice? Blow on it and I'll follow you anywhere."

She laughed. A soft, happy laugh. She sounded as content as a kitten with a fine meal of three mice.

"You're incorrigible but—my sainted mother!—never have I had my fingers around so formidable a man. You're in a class by yourself."

"So they tell me."

I was trying to drive the car, trying to assume an indifference I didn't really feel. It didn't work. Any dame who can do the seventh method is not going to allow a

130

simple little thing like the masturbation bit throw her. Maybe, I wouldn't have to make like Aragoli's bull.

I mooed.

And mooed and mooed.

And she laughed softly and did a thoroughgoing job of attending me. I was wiped dry, recharged, revisited, re-bulleting, and then wiped dry again. I felt ten pounds lighter.

Finally she was satisfied. She nestled against my shoulder once more contentedly. The clouds raced along with the Renault, the sun trying to follow. The road snaked and dipped and dropped between the trees and the hills and the dales. Johnson's man was still in sight.

"It's true," she whispered.

"What is?"

"You are. Your legend, your fame, your reputation. You are indeed the greatest man in America."

"If you say so." From the corner of my eye, I could see, just like in the *living experiments* room, she had gotten some kicks too; the fine stipling of perspiration was across her forehead.

"Rita," I said sternly.

"Yes, Rod."

"I'm going to pound your poop, scratch your snatch and hump you silly when we get to the old dark house."

"I hope so. I'm counting on it. Anything less than that would be a crying shame."

"Crying shame? Lady, you're going to howl your head off."

Her fingers dug into my arm. "Can't you go a little faster then?"

My foot stamped the accelerator to the floorboards and we shot to the rambling, turreted mansion on Parkins Road in ten minutes flat.

But even with sex on my mind and my heart alive with anticipation, I hadn't forgotten that the phone call which had taken me to Ferry Park last night had been a surprisingly inside matter. The telephone voice had known what he shouldn't have.

The caller had known the secret passwords, the May

131

Day and the whole *shmeer*. And how could that have been possible unless the caller was one of us? Of course, the vital information could have been wrung from one of the poor dead kids, prior to total slaughter. I still couldn't forget the terrible going-over they had gotten.

The mansion on Parkins Road loomed in the sunlight, dark, turreted, feudal-looking, like something out of King Arthur's time. The only thing missing was a drawbridge and a moat. And visored guys walking around on the ramparts with halberds poking into the air. It was some layout. The university ought to realize a pretty penny on it when they closed a deal for it.

Rita Cortez was impressed.

A sigh escaped her.

"It will be like days of old, when knights were bold——"

"And toilets weren't invented," I ended it off for her. "Forget it. They got good plumbing here."

"I didn't mean *that*." She almost blushed. "I meant something romantic and——oh, come on, for God's sake, I'm tired of talking about it."

I slammed on the brakes and the Renault rocked to a stop. She squealed in fright. Then laughed.

"Come on, Cortez," I said levelly. "You're about to be conquered."

"I don't want to be conquered. I want to be loved."

"That too," I promised. "All in good time."

"A good time is what I came for."

"This must be the place—in you go, woman. And an obscenity on trading punch lines. I say, let's get this screw on the road."

Her cheeks flamed red but she settled adroitly on my arm and allowed me to hand her out of the car. More and more it looked like I would not need Senor Aragoli's three points.

I had a very big one of my own to make.

The biggest one I've got.

Sunlight warmed our faces as we walked slowly toward the big, old, sprawling mansion on Parkins Road.

132

I felt like we had come for a reading of the will or something.

It was that kind of place.

CHAPTER FOURTEEN

So far so good.

I parked the Renault in a copse of evergreens just to the left of the big front door, making sure the Renault stood out in the sunlight. Rita Cortez, mind made up now and silent as if she were suddenly awed by the rapidity with which our long-awaited confrontation was dawning, kept looking at the ground as I led her up a long, pebbled walk to the house. The landscaping had gone to hell, row upon row of dying, uncared for shrubs looking sickly in the golden light of day. I spotted a couple of broken windows on the wide fieldstone front of the house. I also saw, again out of the corner of my eye, the dark sedan nosing quietly under a big chestnut tree some fifty yards to the right of the structure. Rita didn't see the car. I was happy.

I wasn't only going to get laid. I was going to have police protection while so occupied. The best *Do Not Disturb* sign in the world. Iike a busy call girl who's paid off the local gendarmes to leave her alone.

Rita walked ahead of me into the house after I wrestled with the front door. The key I had was a big, heirloom sort of thing. I tucked it into my pocket after we got inside and re-locked the door. With a bolt and latch, just like in a Karloff movie.

The interior was dim but you could make out the sort of place it must have been with furniture in it. Walnut panel walls looked down on us, big patches of dust-free places on the high sides of the place showed where possible Renoirs, Matisses and Van Goghs might have hung. A fine mist of cobwebs clung to vaulted ceiling and cornices. There was even a broken chandelier dangling from a fixture. Something the former owners had left behind.

A curving, walnut-colored ballustrade rose like a Zeigfeld staircase to the next landing.

"Want to see the rest of the rooms?" I asked.

"Later. Only the bedrooms for now."

"You mean *the* bedroom."

"Yes. Oh, Rod—" There was a catch in her voice.

"Steady. Don't fall down until we find the bed." I knew how she felt though. My heart was hammering like a tom-tom. The call of the wild. I smelled meat. Fresh meat and my nostrils were flaring. If I was a horse I would have whinnied.

"Come on, then," she murmured anxiously. "Take me there. This instant. How much do you think a girl can stand?"

"That's what I'm going to find out."

We didn't need a candle. The sunlight that found its way into the big house was light enough. I followed her up the curving stair, reveling in the gorgeous left-right, left-right, up-down, up-down of her fantastic rear end.

She was shimmering like the pot at the end of the rainbow. A double rainbow like they have in Hawaii. Only mine had two pots.

The upper landing was gloomier, naturally. Which only made things better. Suddenly Rita Cortez halted outside a heavy oaken door I had led her to. Her ivory complexion gleamed in the gloom.

"Wait a minute," she whispered. "It's deserted here. The house is empty. Many bedrooms, you said. But if that's true, there won't be any beds here—"

"Ah, but there is. At least one."

"You bastard," she hissed.

"Who me?"

"Yes, you. You've been here before."

"Certainly. I told you. It's great for—ah—unusual research. I had a bed put in months ago when the Ranselleermans moved out."

"The who?"

"The Ranselleermans. The people who owned the place."

"They sound like a Dutch union of some kind—"

134

"Never mind them. In you go. You'll find everything you'll need or won't need in a wardrobe closet by the bathroom. I laid in some supplies. Just in case."

She tittered and her fragrance was in my flaring nostrils. I pushed her into the room. I did remember to open the door first.

Once inside, she gazed humbly at the gigantic, four-postered antique with high, double-mattress and superb pink sheets and pillows. She chuckled, shaking her head.

"Turn your back," she said. "When you turn around, I shall be ready."

"Don't go away," I replied. But I closed the door and turned my back. All the while I undressed, but quickly, I could hear her making soft, feathery, feminine noises as she did whatever she had to do. I wasn't kidding her about the room. At no small expense to the university, I had had them completely equip the room. With a pile of white rug, soft chairs, et cetera. It was a Playboy layout in an abandoned house. I had performed wonders and learned much in that room. I was about to learn more.

As I stood in the altogether, I was facing the windows. These were French doors leading out to one of the stone terraces that ran around the structure. The picket fence with its rusting iron points that were about ten feet high each stood out at a reasonable distance from the house itself but this one corner bedroom happened to pass almost directly over the picket line as it curved past the second floor. It was a cute gag. I used to tell the dolls that came there they had a fat chance of getting away from me if they changed their minds. I didn't make that crack to Rita Cortez, though. It wasn't necessary. We understood each other.

I think we did.

I don't take off my clothes for just *anybody* who asks me. I didn't imagine she did either.

I waited.

A few minutes ticked by. Wonderful, thrilling, horny seconds in which all I could think of was that splendid body which had first filled my eyes in the *living experiments* room.

135

"*Rod.*"

It was a fierce, low whisper. "Can I turn around now?"

"*Yes.*"

Slowly, I turned. Happily, I faced her. I took a long second to look. I am not the excitable type; I don't have to be in the bedroom league but I knew this was something special.

I tried not to make a smacking sound with my lips. I am never crude.

Rita Cortez stood before me in all of her before-the-dawn-of-Time glory.

Snow White had come out of her shell with a helluva yell. And I was ready to slip her the biggest apple in the world. A whole bushel of apples.

"Take me," she said simply. The green eyes bored into mine as if she absolutely refused to look any lower. I was saluting her the best way I knew how. Front and center. I had almost forgotten just how perfect a wench she was. *Madonna!*

The dark hair glistened in the gloom. The milk-white skin so luminous she might have been wearing clown-paint. The superb spill of her two extraordinary breasts, high, full and firm, thrust out at me inviting me to cup them. The areolas were rosy, pink-tipped, spotted marvelously to seem like another pair of eyes. The taper of her proud torso down to a waistline so trim it only enhanced the bell-shaped flowering of her hips and thighs. Her knees were dimpled. And above and beyond all that and high on the list of goodies were two other items. The nippled navel, so deep and dark and inviting. And last but never least, the exquisite dappling of her convex with its jet black tawny pelt. I was in thrall. I also had an erection that not even Frank Lloyd Wright could have built on his palmiest days.

Before I pole-vaulted across the room to her, I drank my fill. And now, she drank back. Her eyelids fluttered, lowering until her gaze found the stallion of a different hue, make and size. The old pulse jumped in her throat.

"*Madre,*" she breathed. "Why do we wait?"

"Why indeed?" I whispered back and stalked toward

136

her. She made a stand against me and I crashed into her, sweeping her up in my arms, the graceful curves of her great fanny nestling. She pressed her mouth into my left deltoid and bit down. Her small white teeth thrilled me. Thrilled me, chilled me, with a feeling never felt before. Edgar Allan Poe knew what he was talking about. In the girlie department, Rita Cortez was some kind of raven. A stunning big-assed bird, as Alfie might say.

I laid her down on the bed and before she could sink out of sight, I pulled her back. Her thighs widened, and her pelvic muscles jumped. I restrained myself, only a bit longer. We could get down to the fancy tactics later. Right then and there, it was put up or shut up, indeed. With all the soft flesh and prime resiliency of her body, why wait? Time enough later for Yankowski's Method, Dealey's Ploy, Checkerman's Move and Lipschitz's Leap. Right now all I wanted to render Rita Cortez was Rod Damon, *en masse. Tout ensemble* and *oo-la-lala.*

So I screwed her. *A la* Aragoli.

She oohed and aahed, bit into my chest as I hammered down with high glee and hilarity. She threshed and moaned and whimpered and dug fistfuls of empty air as she clawed out in ecstasy. Her toes dug into my sides and she really tried to rear up and throw me off. But she didn't know me well enough yet. I had packed myself inside her so tight she'd have to dynamite me out with a volcanic orgasm.

I didn't notice what was wrong until the first flood that would have sunk Noah's Ark exited from me in a tidal gush of my own pleasure and satisfaction. She shuddered, tensing, trying to hold it all before we overflowed but she had only tapped the barrel. I throbbed like a well-tuned guitar, pouring forth melodies.

But then I noticed.

In spite of her oohs and aahs and twitches, she wasn't comfortable. She was threshing, agitated, not the dance of happy passion. I pulled back to stare down at her. She was damp with me and her own vibrations but pain glowed in the green eyes.

She tried to smile.

137

"What's the matter?" I asked. "Too much too soon?"

She nodded, bravely. "I'm a stupid moron. I'm—uncomfortable. I *hurt* . . . you really are big, you know it?"

"Thank you. Want to take ten? I'm not greedy. We have all day, you know."

"Please. Let's. You lie on your back and let me start this time. Maybe I'm over-prepared or still sore from those fiends at the alley. You do understand? You're not angry?"

"Silly girl. You feel marvelous. Move over. While I regain my own strength."

"Oh, Rod, you're so sweet—" She hugged me, planting my face solidly among her beautiful whim-whams. She smelled fine. I chuckled and dropped over to the other side of the bed and lay back among the pillows. I had made myself happy. I would make her happy once she relaxed. Poor kid. Got carried away, I guess. And popped too soon.

She raised herself to a sitting position, lovely legs draped alongside of me, her feet toward my head. The classic *Soixante-Neuf* beginning in case I got hungry. In the gloom, she was a delightful Venus rising from her wondrous half-shells.

"Rest," she whispered. "Close your eyes. Let Rita do the rest. I want to soothe you. To pour my balm all over you. . . ."

"Balm away." I did as she told me. I closed my eyes and thought happy thoughts. Her body, with its curves and softness, was pretty damn near the whole ball of wax in womankind. Once she hit her stride, I was sure she'd be able to show even me a few things. After all, she knew the Seventh Method, didn't she?

She began to use her mouth again.

My stars, as Clovis Lee would say, she was a miracle. What she could do with her lips and tongue really defies description. But I'll try to tell you anyway.

She started on my ankle, and then my knee. Just feathery pecks and bites and then when I thought she'd stall around awhile longer, she surprised hell out of me. And got heaven in return. She put that suction pump of a

138

mouth of hers right around the top of the head man and blew a tune that I never had heard before. Rapidly, quickly, impossibly fast, I went up up up in her flying machine. She was one Josephine who knew what that old East Indian art is all about. The Continent may have taken it on for its own with French and German variations, but Rita Cortez made it seem like it started in Latin America. She licked clockwise, counterclockwise and cock-wise; I blew my top. Waves of delight and release washed over me. And her. The atmosphere of the room was perfumed with passion.

She got washed along with the tide.

"There," she breathed, in a strangled whisper, still making swallowing sounds. "You incredible man. I have drunk my fill. How do you feel?"

"What a question."

"I hope you're satisfied."

"Sure I am. For about ten minutes. I still owe you about ten of the best."

She managed to laugh, a strange sound in the room. "Oh, perhaps we can do this again sometime. I won't run away. Wait until I'm healed. I'm still sore, I think. I hate to let you down——"

"Let me down?" I rose to put my arms about her, huddling her to my chest. Her damp, dewy flesh was roaring with fire. Only her hands felt cool. "Lady, you let me up. Let me repay you in kind."

"It's not necessary, I told you, Rod. I'm happy. I feel fine—"

"You sure do." I nibbled on her ear, then her neck and my lips moved around to her chin. I kissed that too. And then, with a quick playful dart I bit under her chin right across the slender, fiery column of her throat. She tried to move back, giggling, but I bit into her neck.

Then, in a life of fun, surprises and games, I got THE surprise of my full life. A sudden gift from the Gods, I guess, which might lead me to live awhile longer and still enjoy myself.

I felt with my playful teeth, a strange lump, a funny

139

bump until memory made me remember what the thing was called.

Rita Cortez had an Adam's apple!

Adam's apple, yessirree, Bob.

Like in Steve McQueen.

Like in Peter O'Toole.

Like in Paul Newman.

Like in Richard Burton.

Like in——

Men.

Never like in Sophia Loren.

Or Kim Novak.

Or Raquel Welch.

Or name your own female poison.

Never, never, *never!*

CHAPTER FIFTEEN

While I thought about Adam's rib and how they took one out and made Eve, I also thought about the simple indisputable fact that only men have an Adam's apple and how it represents the core of the forbidden fruit which got stuck going down.

And while I thought in the gloom of that room, Rita Cortez was still making small noises about maybe next time, too tired, still hurting, et cetera. And it all added up to a horrible truth I could no longer endure. Slowly, vigorously, a great burning rage built up inside me.

It all added up now.

Rita Cortez was a sex-switch personality. And that stuck in my throat going down and I almost choked with the realization. Luckily it was gloomy and in the gloom of the room, Rita Cortez could not see my face. If she-he could have, the truth would have spilled the beans. Given the whole thing away.

Everything, from the beginning, had been predicated on my thinking that Rita Cortez was okay. That she was what she seemed. A swell-looking dame who was once a call girl in Puerto Rico. But there was more to it than that—

"Rod?"

"Still here."

"You seem miles away—you're sure you're not angry?"

"Me? The idea."

She had been lousy in bed. If I hadn't been so horny I could have known that right away. She did everything else right. The erotic play like the seventh method. The *fellatio*. The moves, the patter. But that was all. Straight Sex was uncomfortable. What a surprise.

She had beautiful boobs, a delicate velvety vagina, a perfectly shapely derrière, a hot tongue and a skin as soft and white as snow. But her heart was blacker than any Wicked Queen's. She was the traitor in our midst; she was the Judas. And somewhere along the line, she had been responsible for the deaths of six swell kids. The Glee Club, hah. That had to be a phony routine. Or her own private Gestapo.

Even as my mind weighed all these glaring truths, I knew what I had to do. And fast. He-she, or whatever the hell she was, was going to produce the Truth, if she couldn't produce anything else. I hadn't run into that many Copenhagen types before and my interest was far from scientific.

All I wanted was the real Truth and I was mad enough to get it the only way possible.

"Rod, what are you doing?" There was sudden alarm in her blurt as I took her by the shoulders and forced her down to the pillows. None too gently.

"I'm sorry, baby. Just one more turn around the block?"

"Oh, you!" She sounded as feminine as hell protesting. What a laugh. "Come on, now, Rod. I told you. Next time, all right, my darling? I'm so fatigued—"

"Aw, come on."

"No, please—" She tried to ease out from beneath me, but I had her straddled, the still incredible thighs and extra delights pinned beneath me, wide open for the kill.

"Now, Rita . . . just a little more . . ."

She cried out. I couldn't blame her. Fury does strange

141

things to me. When love and affection are not wrapped up in my work, I'm as hard as a branding iron and twice as smoking. Purposefulness, other than working off my excess heat, were firing my brain. She was very distasteful to me now. I only knew one thing, though. Straight Sex being uncomfortable for Rita Cortez, it followed as the night the day that I could hurt her very much with a pecker that had no love for her. Also, I might learn a lot more.

"Rod! Don't—that hurts!"

"Splendid. How's *that?*"

"Oh, no—*madre*, you are—please, stop—"

So I pounded all the harder. From the top. With all my weight, fury, hate and private reasons. I rose and fell like a battering ram, thundering into her softness and non-cooperative twitching. She cried out in mingled ecstasy and agony and all I could do was Go, Go, Go! Her nails raked my back, my ass; she thudded her fists into my chest. But I had my teeth clenched, my flaps out and my landing gear down. I was coming in for a crash landing. I knew she couldn't take it. Few dames could have taken it, stood up to such an assault. With the kind of operation Rita Cortez had had once, regardless of how long ago it might have been, such a screwing can't be easy.

She cried out in terror, now. I was heedless to it all. If I had had any qualms, compunctions or second thoughts, all I had to remember was what she had done, or had *had* done to Doreen Doremus, Corinne Murphy, Alice Potter, Norma Davis and Adele Ash. And Tony Eden.

So it was easy to be cruel to her. She had it coming.

I got so wrapped up in my spite work, so insanely concentrative on my thrust, I lost all track of time. Lost all perspective. I never did feel the feebleness of Rita Cortez's thudding fists, the gradual slowing down of her twitching body, the pitiful moaning of her voice. Not until I gathered all my muscle, reared on high and came down with one more thundering bombardment that had no orgasm in it—nothing but hatred and fury and firmness the thickness and texture of a bung-starter, did I know I had won.

142

She let out one long whimpering bleat and collapsed beneath me. Like a wet rug. There was no more fight in her. She might have been dead. But she wasn't.

Only unconscious.

Only out for the count.

I'd like to have left her for Count Dracula but I had things to do. Things to do that a vampire might have gotten some kicks out of. But very necessary. And right up a ghoul's alley.

La Cortez was limp, damp and almost dead from a screwing few mortals could have survived. But it accomplished my two purposes. The first one which had been to punish her. The second—to examine her.

Walrus-moustache has taught me a lot about the art of spying. The tricks of agents the world over. Also, I remembered his story about Marlene Rakovny in the shootout in Frisco and the sealed orders found in her bra. Agents always carry sealed orders. So I didn't expect to find them on Rita Cortez's clothes. Not the one yard of fabric she had called a dress. Now that she was naked, there was only one place to look. I was sure Rita Cortez had her instructions, too. And considering the incredible twist of medical science that had made a beautiful woman out of a man, it was the only place worth considering. Dames trying to smuggle heroin and high-priced jewelry through Customs always use that place. Either concealed in a stick of Tampon or just simple storage. It was worth a gamble, as messy as it might be.

I didn't have to look.

In the dark, I thrust my fingers into her crevice, searched around until the tips of my fingers made contact with something small, smooth and pellet-like. I yanked it out. Rita Cortez did not stir. Not so much as a moan. I walked to the French doors, opened them to let the sunlight in and examined my find. First, I brushed it clean on one of the curtains draping the glass.

The sunlight told me all.

I was holding a spool—a cylinder of possibly microfilm. It sure as hell wasn't a birth control pill or an intrauterine device. I do know what those look like. I felt

143

mildly exultant. I was sure this would provide the possible answer to what Walrus-moustache needed to know. Rita Cortez just had to be one of the biggest fishes in the school of enemy sharks swimming in the American waters.

I lead a charmed life. I must. There I was standing bare-assed naked on the terrace, like Adam in the sunlight and the shot rang out. A clean, clear whip of sound cutting across the area surrounding the old house and the bullet missed by only about an inch. It zinged past my head and splintered one of the panes of glass in the French windows. I ducked. For a moment, I thought Rita Cortez had roused herself, found the .32 I had brought with me and tried to shoot me in the back. But, no. Someone was taking target practice from a tall chestnut tree just about thirty feet from the iron picket fence. I got back inside as another shot sang out.

I got the gun, checked it for firing and dashed back out to the terrace, keeping low. The patio was bordered by a stone railing with ballusters about half a foot thick in the shape of Doric columns. I squinted in the sunlight, looking toward the chestnut tree. I didn't have to wait long. Whoever was out there wanted me bad. Another shot came spanging off the stone about a foot from my face. I caught the gleam of a gun barrel in the sunlight. I have a good eye. Not only for women. I sighted along the balluster I was behind, took careful aim and managed to squeeze off one shot. Maybe I was lucky, again. Who knows?

There was a sudden scream of sound, a threshing among the branches of the big tree and then a body began to thump, thump, thump, down from an outstretched limb until it slammed into the earth out of sight. Bingo. On the first shot.

It couldn't have been Johnson's man. Cops don't make like snipers in that kind of situation. Could I have been wrong all along? Was the tail that had followed us from the university not the same one that had trailed me from the police station? Or was the answer simpler than that— that Johnson also had a spy in his midst, one of his own

144

men on the take from the Red Chinese? All things are possible in a double-dealing world.

Boy, are they ever!

The sniper had missed but he accomplished something. The shooting awakened Rita Cortez and the next thing I knew she had come rushing from the bedroom. I didn't see her face right away. Because the first time I knew she was back among us was the swinging blow that nearly took my fool head off.

Bells clanged, drums thundered and I tried to get out of the way. She came charging by, my dodge making her miss me. She came up against the stone parapet and whirled. Now I really got a good look at her. For a long moment, confrontation made us both look at each other.

How can I explain it?

There she was. A gorgeous woman, everything going for her. Skin, hair, eyes—those green eyes!—and all that splendid equipment in equal parts. The breasts, the hips, the thighs, the Snow White flesh. That Venus mound of enticement. But she wasn't a dame—she was a guy. A guy who still had her Adam's apple and the brain, mind and psyche of a man who wanted to be a spy for a living. Not a man—or a woman, really, for that matter. Twisted, like I tell you.

She came toward me, arms out like a Japanese Sumo wrestler, body alert and tensed. Maybe I had worn her out in the sack, but she looked as fit as a fiddle and ready to play games. Games like let-me-kill-you-with-my-bare-hands. I dropped back warily. I was tired too. And there was no place to run. This was it. Showdown and Payoff Day.

"You arch cock-proud bastard," she hissed. "Do you know what I'm going to do with you when you're in my power?"

"Let me guess, you real double agent," I hissed back, backing off. "I've seen your homework. Why did you kill those poor kids like that?"

"A pleasure." She showed me her teeth and shot out her right hand in an experimental Karate slice. It whistled past my face and I weaved to the other side of the bal-

145

cony. "I enjoyed it, you hear? All of it. Fat Ass, Corinne, Adele—the others. And Tony Eden—if he'd been a real man he would have gotten his operation too instead of being half-and-half. . . ." Her left foot lashed out in a *Savate* kick. I tried to grab it and missed and she came running back slapping out both hands in a rapid series of chopping punches. I struck out with a right cross but she laughed and ducked back. Her footwork was incredible. A Black Belt expert at the very least. In Karate, Kendo, Kado and you name it. I began to sweat in the sun. I hadn't expected her to have muscles *too*.

"That scene you staged in the bowling alley. A lie, wasn't it?" I panted. "There was no Glee Club. That was something you thought up to throw me off. So I wouldn't expect you to be a spy. Not someone who had been brutally raped—you're good, kid. Like using the seventh method on me in front of the whole class and on film, to prove you were a woman. Instead of a queer-bastard-spy pervert who could do insane things to six poor kids who never hurt a fly in their lives."

"Damon," she said, coming closer slowly. The green eyes were insane, now. "I killed your students because China is all to me. They paid for my operation. Yes, I hired some local boys from town to fake the bowling alley scene. What of it? I needed no help to take care of Fat Ass Doreen. And Corinne. And Alice and Norma and Adele and Tony. They all wanted to be spies. Hah! They couldn't have found honey in a beehive. Yes, I took care of all of them by myself. All I needed was a bottle to simulate the rapes. The effects are the same I can assure you."

"You bitch—bastard." I tried to slug him-her but she danced out of the way again, snarling. "Where's your Bowie knife? I'd like to stick it up you until it comes out the other side. But killing's too good for you."

"You say. But never mind that, Damon. I want you, now. My way. You may have killed my assistant, Rod—the one in the tree who provided me with dead Russian agents to leave as calling cards—but you—you I take care of personally . . ."

The talking to me was a trap. She had tried to lull me.

146

That was very obvious. Because she was done talking. She let out a low tigerish cry of the jungle and rushed me. Swarming all over me like a band of monkeys. She came with all her goodies swinging, and if anybody in a helicopter was watching the fight, he would have sworn off the bottle or crashed into a tree with shock.

A naked man and a naked woman, like Adam and Eve in the good old days going at it hammer and tongs.

I had forgotten all about the pellet of microfilm or whatever the hell it really was. It lay abandoned somewhere on the terrace. Neither Rita Cortez or I had paid any attention to it.

Who could with his testicles about to be kicked to smithereens?

Because that was exactly what Rita Cortez was trying to do. My fanny was getting bruised and scratched backing away from her darting feet as I brushed against the exterior of the house.

I couldn't get a hold on her slippery, greased-lightning body. She moved like a ferret, whipping in and out of charges and crouches. I was losing wind, heart and hope. After all, I'm only human after all. The sex switch named Rita Cortez was inhuman. Subhuman. Like a beast of the field.

Fagged out, I fell back. She was between me and the safety of the French doors now. Limned against their gloom with her snow-white figure, she could have stepped out of a man's wildest fantasies. But she was one of Nature's cheats. A double person, a double agent. A killer and a terrorist both.

"Damon—*die!*"

She came at me headlong. I tried to get out of the way. But her right foot crashed into my shoulder and I went down. As I crumpled, she shot over me, wanting to come back for a savage Half-Nelson kind of hold that would have broken my neck, the shape I was in. Desperately I flung an arm up, hooked it into her gut and heaved. Upward and outward. The flying momentum of her superb figure was not to be denied. And who am I to stand in the way of the laws of unchangeable, immutable phys-

147

ics? I am only a great lover, after all. But a little *Jiu Jitsu* goes a long way.

She screamed. Just once. Her hurtling, rushing figure sailed over my battered head, cleared the stone parapet by a full foot and before she could check her flight, down she went. I heard a long, trailing screech of terror and then abruptly, like the turning of another kind of switch, screech, fall, terror all came to a thudding halt. Silence. Broken only by the sudden fluttering of frightened birds in the trees that flanked the old house.

I reeled to my feet. Dazed, battered, even bleeding as I found out later. She had opened a six-inch gash along my left jawbone. And my right eye was turning purple.

But you should have seen the other guy. Girl. Aw, hell.

I stared down over the stone parapet.

I did not look away.

Not even the screwing I had given Rita Cortez could match the one she had gotten from the high iron picket fence that ran around the property that the university owned.

Yeah, verily, in the vernacular of King Arthur and his crowd.

She had dropped like a rock, on target, and one of the rustiest, sharpest pickets poking into the sky had keyed her lock forever. Right up into her whatsit, as Johnson might say.

She hadn't even had time for a single dying twitch. Death must have been instantaneous. But I didn't shed one single tear for her. She had had it coming to her. All the way up.

And down.

Let the Devil cry for her. I wasn't going to. I had gotten some of my own back at last. And I hoped devoutly that six swell college kids were all having a high old horse-laugh somewhere.

I looked for the microfilm, found it and carried it back into the bedroom with me. I got dressed slowly, aware of every single new ache and muscle I had found within the last hour or so. I wasn't going to clean up. Johnson could do that. The deal was closed as far as I was con-

148

cerned. Dead spies all over the place. Red Chinese folde-rol. Hooey. I longed for the university and my research and my willing panting student body. Rod Damon, Secret Agent. I really had to laugh. It is definitely not my line of work. Or endeavor.

Does Richard Burton work for the Peace Corps?

Certainly not! Liz wouldn't stand for it.

CHAPTER SIXTEEN

A day later I went to see Walrus-moustache in the hospital. He had come out of his coma, screaming for information and his clothes. Once a cop, always a cop. The policeman instinct is worse than a case of the hives. You should have seen Johnson when he finally came out to the house on Parkins Road after I called in. They needed a derrick to get Rita Cortez's corpse off the picket fence. The guy I had shot out of the tree was a character named Fergis O'Sullivan whom the world of the city had thought of as a harmless Irish drunk who hung around bars. Actually he turned out to be a real Ivan. Ivan Korky, top hatchet man for the Hanoi crowd and working hand-in-glove with Rita. But there was so much more to know. So much to learn. I had sent the microfilm to the Coxe Foundation and waited for them to tell me what it con-tained. But they didn't, so I was sure Walrus-moustache would have the answers I needed. He did. He knows *everything*. Bad crack on the noggin and all. I wouldn't tell him to his face but I was glad he was alive. Some people you really miss, even your worst enemies. They add spice and variety to life. You know, like a shack-up with two women in the same bed. Or don't you know?

"Ah, Damon. Good of you to come."

"I always come. It's my specialty, remember. Now, give, you old pirate. I am entitled to some answers, don't you think?"

"Certainly, my boy." He was feeling chipper and mag-nanimous, I could see. Sitting up in bed, swathed in head bandages, his big moustache bristling and shining as if it had been freshly scrubbed. "By all means. Where shall I start?"

"With the microfilm I found on Rita Cortez."

He positively glowed with pride. "Microdot, Damon. The very latest thing. And may I say once again, I am proud of you, Damon. I know how costly this enterprise has been to you personally. All those charming young people of yours but your work this time is an inspiration to us all. Devotion to service and duty—extraordinary. Gad, how did you tumble that the Cortez woman was a sex change type?"

"The usual way. But my methods are my own."

"Indubitably."

"Now how about the microdot—please?"

"Yes, of course." His moustache twitched and he shuddered. "Ghastly. When I think how close we came to disaster—Damon, here it is. The microdot was more powerful than even you can imagine."

"Try me. I've got an hour before I go back to school for my classes."

"All right, my boy. I'll get to it. Simply, horribly, the plan was this. It's all there on the microdot, a top priority code plan for the project. A directive for disaster—" He is long-winded but he finally gets to the point. Sooner or later. "Your Rita Cortez was to alert all Chinese and Albanian agents in the area to help her kidnap the Russian ambassador to the United States. This was a detail even more important than the trafficking of new agents into this country. It seems the plot was to have the Russian ambassador turn up dead in the rooms of your university. In a sexual, orgiastic manner which would both shock and horrify the sensibilities and decorum of we horrible capitalists and embarrass the peaceful nations of the world at large. You see?"

"I think so. A feather in the Red Chinese cap, a black eye for the Commies and us and China plays even a bigger hand at the UN?"

"Precisely. You are getting up on your political intelligence, Damon. I am pleased. With such a horror in the world press, quite like Hitler's excuses in Czechoslovakia

150

and Poland, China would win lots of brownie points. Like say, kicking the Caucasians out of Asia, grabbing Siberia for themselves. Simple, really, but certainly a giant step in their master plan to run the world one day-that-will-live-in-infamy from now."

I cracked my knuckles. Walrus-moustache winced.

"I see. One transvestite named Rita Cortez almost upset the international apple cart. That *balance*, you were talking about."

"Quite. It was her own plan, as near as we can make out. She must have talked her employers into the scheme. And please don't crack your knuckles, old boy. My head aches most fearfully."

"You horny old wolf," I growled. "I ought to hit you in the head myself. Why did you take Adele Ash to that motel?"

He sobered up immediately. And I felt sorry for him.

"I am sorry about that, Damon. I confess I was carried away with her beauty. Her freshness, her—you know I had the same notion you had with Cortez. I wanted to flush out some spies. I didn't mean it to end the way it did."

"Did you make her happy at least before the roof fell in?"

His head jerked erect. He stared at me without wincing. He looked so damn nobly grotesque with his bandages I had to smile.

"Don't laugh at me, Damon. Yes, I made Adele happy. And she made me happy. And then while we were resting in each other's arms, they got the drop on us. Cortez and that damn accomplice of hers, Korky. He I knew. I didn't realize who she was until Chief Johnson told me about the spiked fence. I had never met her, you see."

"But you had guessed that the double agent might be a woman? That thing you yelled out in Cabin Number Nine. The owner, what's-his-name Oregano heard you shout something about it being a girl."

Walrus-moustache frowned.

"Really? How excessively odd. I don't know what you mean. I never said that. We had the TV on in the cabin.

151

Watching a movie. Some comedy film. Are you sure? I do remember I got out of bed to turn the set down. That's when we were jumped—"

I shook my head. So much for great murder cases and how they are solved. My biggest clue, hottest lead and it all had come from a TV set tuned up! Put that in your Sherlock Holmes and smoke it!

"Well," I said. "I hope the suntanned and windburned bastards stop coming in. I got work to do. Am I off the case, now? There's my research. Three coeds I promised an experiment and you know me—"

"My boy," he said expansively. "You can have anything you ask. I am empowered to congratulate you. By the Foundation—and to wish you nothing but the best. By all means, go back to your books and studies, Damon. Crack a few tomes for me."

"Thank you. Rest easy. Any idea when you'll be crashing this hotel?"

"Day or two. No more than that."

"Good. Maybe I'll send you one of my students to hold your hot hand and read to you. Would you like that?"

His eyes glowed again. "Really, old man? Would you? I would like that, I think. Your students are all so—charming."

"The live ones are," I agreed. "Well, *caio*. See you in the funny papers. You, of course, know that it was Rita Cortez who phoned us that night in my rooms and used a disguised voice to send me off to Ferry Park?"

"*Caio,* Damon." His wave wâs feeble. "And I expect you know that she had *The Alarm Clock* burned to the ground as another diversion for us to think about. Perhaps, she was destroying some evidence. Who *does* know?"

"It figured—" I headed for the door.

"Oh, Damon."

"Yeah?"

"When that woman made her bogus call, you went like a brave man. Never once hesitated. You *are* the greatest Coxeman of us all."

"You'd better believe it," I said and left.

I could hear him chuckling as I closed the door.

152

Pete Porter was waiting for me in front of the building.

I'd brought him down with me in the Renault because it was a lousy time for him to be all by his lonesome. He was as big and bronzed as ever but he needed the company. He grinned happily when he saw me, as if he didn't have a care in the world. As if he hadn't lost six of his best friends. I'm not counting Rita Cortez.

I let him drive. It was good for him to be doing something.

On the way to the university, I asked him to stop by the police station. I wanted to say goodbye to Johnson. Who was also happy that the great sex crime wave was over.

Who wasn't?

Johnson was in.

Looking like he'd recovered some of his lost youth. His hair was nicely combed and he almost looked as if he was humming. Success in a murder case can do that for a cop. Pete Porter shouldered into the room behind me.

Johnson was happy to see me. Even though he was still a wee bit red-faced about how his man who had tailed me had bolixed the job. Cortez's minion, Korky, had successfully let the air out of the tires of his car so that he could himself tail me in peace.

"Greetings, Johnson. Thought I'd just stop by to rub it in some more. About how Sex isn't the only thing I'm any good at. Wouldn't you agree?"

"Professor! Have a chair. Have two chairs. Always glad to see a great detective. Hi, son——" He gestured Pete Porter to a seat. "You all must be proud of Damon here. A regular James Bond!"

Porter chuckled. "That isn't all he is. You should see him in the living experiments room with three dames——"

"Pete, please." I looked at Johnson. "You carrying a gun?"

He laughed. "You kidding? Of course. Right here." He patted his hip where a .38 pistol rode. "What's the idea?"

"May I see it a minute, please? I can tell you how Rita Cortez was able to kill and butcher six students and two Russian agents."

153

He frowned, shrugged, but he was a cop too. He handed the .38 across the desk. I took it, balanced it in the palm of my hand and then turned around and pointed it right at Pete Porter's face. He grinned and put his hands up. "You got me, Prof. What's the gag?"

Johnson half rose behind the desk. "Easy, Professor. That thing's loaded."

"I know it is," I said, still looking at big, handsome Pete Porter. "I hope it is. I'm loaded too. Loaded with hate and rage for a bastard like him who helped kill six people he went to school with and maybe made love to and I am including Tony Eden. Tell us about it, Pete, before I blow your brains out."

The blood drained from his grin and he looked mad too.

"Cut it out, Prof. Put that gun down. You loco? Me kill anybody? My pals——"

"Johnson," I said, without taking my eyes off Pete Porter. "Rita Cortez was a man who became a woman, courtesy Copenhagen. She was strong, but she was only five feet five and weighed maybe one hundred and eighteen pounds wringing wet. She killed. She did all the slicing, all the brutality. But I tell you she needed a man to help pin down a big heifer like Doreen, to tie up a six-foot woman like Adele Ash and to manhandle girls like Alice Potter and Corinne Murphy and Norma Davis. And Tony Eden—Tony was six two and weighed two hundred——"

"We know all that," Johnson growled. "Wasn't Korky her man Friday? He helped to do the muscle work——"

"No," I said. "Pete Porter did. Pete who lured Alice and Norma to that park. Who helped put that agent up in Washington's boat. Rita Cortez couldn't have managed, nor could Korky. He was small enough to hide in a tree and fall out of it almost without me seeing him. And I was there the night Pete came puffing up telling me how his car ran out of gas thanks to a hole in the tank. Come on, Pete. Confession's good for the soul. On the take from China, huh? You either tell me or I'm going to put a hole right where your manhood now is. I won't kill you; I'll just fix you so you won't be good for a woman again."

154

He was white as a sheet. His hands trembled in the air. He looked at Johnson and then at me again. His eyes were almost wet with tears.

"Prof, you're crazy! This is me, Pete. Your student. I didn't do any of those things you said. How could I?"

"Pete, I'm going to shoot. I don't care what you say. You don't talk, it doesn't matter—your wang isn't going to be good enough for anything." I leveled the gun at his crotch. Johnson swore but he couldn't do a thing. Pete saw that. His chin sagged. I pulled back the hammer of the pistol. It clicked.

And Pete Porter collapsed.

"Okay, okay—don't shoot—goddamnit, don't shoot—I was in on it with Rita Cortez—I'm a special agent for China—anything—but don't shoot—I had to do it—I've got a brother who is their prisoner in Chungking. I had to cooperate." He started to sway.

I smiled, walked toward him, raised the gun and slammed it into his forehead. He went backwards, taking a chair with him and lay on the floor like a big rug. Out cold. I handed the gun back to Johnson, who could only stare, his mouth drooping.

I sat down, took out my cigarettes and lit one up. Johnson shook himself. He took his eyes off Pete Porter and stared at me now.

"You were bluffing."

"Not really. Cortez is small. Was, that is. Korky's no muscle man. Someone had to have helped Rita on the inside and with the details. Since Pete was the only one left of my original team, what's to bluff? It had to be him."

"Did you kill him? He looks poleaxed."

"He'll live. The others won't. When he comes to, you tell him how close he came to getting his balls shot off. I wanted to mark him up. Mark him for life."

Johnson rebuttoned the flap on his holster.

"My hat's off to you, Professor. You got the makings of a real cop. Delivering him down here and all. Why are you wasting your time on this Sexology and all that L.S.D. you mentioned?"

"Are you kidding? It's the only way to fly."

155

"I ought to give you an honorary rating with this department. You got it coming. I'll talk to the mayor about it, okay?"

"You do that." I stood up, shook hands with him and left the office. I didn't give Pete Porter a second look. The fink. Brother or no brother, he was the rat of all time in my book. Even worse than Rita Cortez. Rita was a double person and a double agent, but Pete Porter was a double fink.

I drove back to the university in a very thoughtful mood. The blue sky and hot sun kept me company; for once, I had nothing on my mind. No, not even Sex. I was bushed, tired, flagged out, fagged out and pooped. I needed a vacation for all time, from all things. Or so I thought. I always threaten to reform but something's always happening.

There was a hitchhiker on the highway. Standing next to a blue Buick with a radiator front that had made contact with a tall tree just over the next bend on the lane. I slowed down.

The hitchhiker was about 38-24-38, with a blue tam, yellow sweater and blue skirt. The top thirty-eight was proud, the twenty-four was compact and the other thirty-eight was a wriggling symmetry not seen since the days of Monroe. Marilyn, that is.

"Oh," she wailed, running toward me, all points jiggling delightfully. Her mouth was red, her eyes blue and the red hair looked fiery in the haze of day. "I'm so glad you stopped. I have to get to the university by one o'clock and it's almost that now—you're ever so kind."

"I'll take you," I said. "It's my next stop, Miss—"

"Lee," she said, gratefully, crowding next to me in the Renault, all honey and accent. "Deborah Lee. My sister is enrolled there and she doesn't know it, but I signed up too. You see she's been writing me about this wonderful Professor they have there. And all the thrilling and exciting things he shows them and tells them. And does. I had to *come*. . . ." Appeal shot out of the blue eyes. She was a pippin, all right.

"You will," I promised fervently, feeling the old battle

156

cry in my blood. My kind of fever. "Hang on, Deborah Lee. *Away* we go!"

Which is how Deborah Lee came to the university to become a vital part of my curriculum. And sexual research.

I was able to expand and develop more fully all my notes and data and related materials on the very delicate and ticklish subject: *Sibling Syndrome, Its Cause and Effect on the Sex Act Both Individually and in Tandem with the Same Sex Partner.*

Sheesh.

Clovis' little sister, exactly nine months younger, was a honeyed revelation. Clovis had to go along with the gag. Or else she would have been left out in the cold. What the hell. She enjoyed herself as much *ménage-à-trois* as the next girl. It doesn't hurt to share the wealth, you know. One of the primary rules of sexual amusement and entertainment. Love is something else again.

It has to be. But I don't travel that route. I don't have to and I can't. Nature made me what I am today. Ask the girls. Ask the student body of the university.

Anyone I have ever socked it to knows that.

And it's all *very interesting*.

As Walrus-moustache is my judge.

What the hell, no matter what I am and what I do, I did solve the Great Spy Influx Mystery. All with my little bow and arrow. Little? Pshaw.

Leave us not be ridiculous.

We, Damon and Company, are still kings of the hill, the biggest bucks in the lick.

And the beauty of it is, I never took a lesson in my life.

CHAPTER SEVENTEEN

"You intelligent females know what you have to do now?" I asked one night, a week later.

Both Clovis Lee and Deborah Lee nodded. We were alone in the big bedroom at the old dark house on Parkins

157

Road. But it was a different time, a different type of female. And the big bed was intact. So was the room, the French doors and the glorious sunlight. It had been a nice season of weather all around. Walrus-moustache was back among the record files at the Thaddeus X. Coxe Foundation.

I was enjoying my freedom.

I was naked and so were Clovis and Deborah. They were both lying on the big bed, facing the ceiling. Ravishing redheads. A set.

"Oh," Clovis murmured, "what is on that cunning mind of yours, Rod?"

"Hush, Clovis Lee," Deborah Lee said admiringly. "You leave him alone. Can't you see he's thinking and this is mighty important?"

She was that kind of girl. A real fan. I could do no wrong. After all I was six feet, one hundred and eighty pounds, handsome and an authority on a subject she had a boundless interest in. And I came equipped with that built-in miracle of my own, which was now standing out for inspection and truly remarkable. Sometimes it gets even me awed.

I lay down between them, feeling their splendid mounds walling me in. I too looked at the ceiling. We were all as quiet as mice. We hardly breathed. But I could feel the electricity in the room. The fire of the flesh, the thrill of anticipation. It gets you everytime. And *them*.

"Remember the rules now," I reminded them. "Nobody talks. Nobody looks at the other person. This ploy is called *Hesitation*. They have found it most beneficial in psychotherapy where the frigid person is still inhibited and uptight. Actually, however, couples that don't have that problem can add it to their bag of tricks as another innovation for inducing desire and refreshing their sexual taste buds, as it were. Like, say, a couple who've been balling for years and have lost all their approach technique. Gone stale, you know."

I could feel their nods.

"What do we do?" Clovis whispered.

158

"You do what you want. Hands, toes, rubbing—anything—just don't rush it. Ready now?"

"*Yay-yussss*," Deborah cooed.

"Uh huh," Clovis sighed.

"Then go."

We went.

Slowly, softly, quietly. Clovis' hand strayed toward my family jewels. Deborah's cool hand splayed across my stomach. My both feet worked along their ankles, up and down. Within minutes, we were all fired up.

The girls couldn't hold out.

Clovis lost her head.

Deborah got impatient.

The experiment was a failure. I had hoped for too much and not accounted for the magic of the Damon weapon. It gets them everytime. After all, a female in heat isn't going to tease herself mad if she doesn't have to. Especially redheads. Remember what I said about them?

So Clovis fell over me, wolfing, gulping, splattering me with juicy moist kisses. And then Deborah wanted her share just like big sister and before I know what happened just then, the three of us were roiling and rolling in a mad tangle of three that had no beginning and no ending. So much for the Hesitation Ploy. What the hey. It didn't matter. The bed was big enough and I wasn't that interested in research that fine afternoon.

What a darling combination of arms, legs, toes and important tendons we made. It didn't seem to matter who was on top or on bottom. It was a mad, delightful private little orgy and we had the wilderness of the countryside to ourselves. That and the gloomy wonder of the vast bedroom.

I rocked, they rolled.

I rolled, they rocked.

I changed hands and so did they.

I changed weapons and so did they.

Quite a democracy we had going. And nobody got mean or selfish or greedy. I guess there was enough to go around. Enough for all, with seconds and thirds to spare. Maybe that's the whole secret of peace in our time.

159

Maybe Walrus-moustache and the Coxe Foundation ought to tell that to Red China. And anybody else that needs the lesson.

Clovis Lee came up, damp with enthusiasm, on fire with passion, and blew a lock of hair out of her eyes. She looked tousled and magnificent.

"Oh, Professor—" she breathed fiercely. She could say no more and went down again. Busy little beaver with teeth to match.

Deborah Lee bobbed into view, licking her lips, looking balled and beautiful. Her flaming hair was sprawling and so were her lively twin boobs. They were dangling harmoniously.

"Rodney, honey—you are *the* most—" And down she went too to divide the spoils with sister Clovis. Bringing flamethrowers with her.

I sighed contentedly.

Damn me, it *was* the truth, wasn't it?

After all, *who* is the Greatest Coxeman of them all?

Nobody but little old me.

They'll tell you that in Red China, too.